C0-DVG-139

*The
Enigma
of
Out-of-Body
Travel*

53277

BY SUSY SMITH

The Enigma of Out-of-Body Travel

Gellert Memorial Library
St. Paul's Seminary & University
DISCARD

HELIX PRESS / *Garrett Publications* / NEW YORK

CMenSP

BF
1389
A7 S6

Copyright © 1965 by Susy Smith
Library of Congress Catalog Card No. 65-18998
Designed by David Miller
Manufactured in the United States of America

to Professor C. J. Ducasse

for his

great wisdom

and kindness.

Contents

The
Enigma
of
Out-of-Body
Travel

I

An Introduction to the Subject

WAS SHE REALLY FLOATING IN THE AIR AS SHE SEEMED TO BE?
Or had she died and gone to heaven? Fourteen-year-old Mary
Sharpe knew this was not death as she understood it, so she
must be alive. But if she was, then something mighty strange
was happening. Her conscious mind was travelling away from
her body, which lay quietly on the bed in her room.

"My first impression," Mary said (somewhat later, be it
understood), "was of floating backwards, as if resting on the
great beautiful blue clouds I saw all around me. On them I
soared up and up and *up!*"

Actually, she was near to death. It was July, 1903, when this
Stillwater, Minnesota, woman was a teenage girl, and she had
lapsed into a coma some minutes before. Then she found
herself high on those clouds of blue, which gradually changed
to lavender and pink. Finally she was completely bathed in
golden light.

It was then that a man appeared beside her. As she recalls it now, "He seemed to be buoying me up—as one might
a swimmer learning to float. I saw his face and his hair, which
was a light brown tinged a little with gold." She does not
recall that he spoke to her, but in some manner his name was
conveyed to her. It was Edwin Emeny.

Mary turned her head and looked back down over her
right shoulder at the room she had left. It appeared as if in

miniature far below her. She could see the whole room in detail; but something looked different to her—her body was reversed on the bed. She learned later that after she had gone into the comatose condition she had been turned around and her head placed at the foot of the bed so that she might get the cool breeze from the window. Mary could see her mother standing beside the bed, together with another woman and a strange man. (They were the anxious doctors attending her—Dr. Cora Emeny, her family physician, and Dr. Henry Fullerton, who had just been called in for consultation.)

Her mother's despair at her condition seemed to draw Mary back, and she returned from her cloudswept paradise; but, she says, "On reaching my body I didn't quite hit the shoulders just right, and I scrunched them, as one does to fit into a coat." This shrugging motion was the first sign of life she had shown for some time, and her mother and the doctors were delighted. Soon she opened her eyes, and asked for a drink of water. Then she fell into a natural sleep, and from that time on her health improved.

Several days later Mary Sharpe asked Dr. Cora Emeny who Edwin Emeny was.

"Edwin Emeny? Where did you get that name?" the doctor asked.

"Why, that was the name of the man I saw up there." She had already spoken of her flight, but so far no one had paid much attention to her. "He looked very much like you," she added.

"You saw his face?"

"Oh, yes. And his hair was just the same shade as yours, too."

The doctor turned to Mary's mother, and her voice shook as she said, "My brother Edwin has been dead fifteen years. How could the child have known his name, or how he looked? I have never mentioned him here."

After this Mary's family was inclined to listen a little more respectfully to her ramblings about her strange travel during her illness. But even so, she was to learn not to speak of it. Although an incident of great significance to her, for it gave her an intimation that there was something within her body which might be able to escape it at death and soar away on clouds of blue and gold, she found others extremely reluctant to hear about it. Out-of-body experiences have not yet become the fashion.

"When I have told this story through the years," says Mary, who is now in her seventies, "some people acted as if I were slightly daft."

However, there are increasingly fewer who respond in such a manner. The idea that some individuals can live and function consciously for a time outside their physical bodies is startling, to say the least; but we just aren't as alarmed by the incomprehensible nowadays. The atom has been split. We have been told by atomic physicists that our own bodies, as well as all other matter, are composed almost entirely of empty space; and if we can believe this we can believe anything.

Science fiction is turning out to be more science than fiction. Far-out television shows which make claims of authenticity for their fanciful stories are becoming commonplace. While we may occasionally, and rightly, credit their bizarre character to poor scripts, we nonetheless are beginning to realize that no inventive imagination can be more fantastic than fact.

And so, the general public is growing aware that there are legitimate events, such as the out-of-body experiences we are discussing, which are not explainable by the laws of nature as we now understand them. Miss Sharpe is today more likely to be thought merely pleasantly eccentric than "daft."

Even so, the reader may ask why one should take such accounts seriously enough to write a book about them. This is primarily because of the enormous number of such incidents reported, and their similarity. Individuals who know nothing about anyone else's analogous experiences will independently give almost identical accounts of their own. Such reports are so widespread—acròss the world, and from the dawn of time —that they cannot be ignored.

"But," the reader may say, "nobody I know has anything like that happen to him." This, of course, may not be true. Persons who have undergone such weird adventures are extremely reluctant to speak of them unless they are absolutely sure they will not be rebuffed or laughed at. Like Mary Sharpe, they don't want to be called daft.

A prominent psychical researcher of the early part of this century, Dr. Walter Franklin Prince, has pointed out that people will talk about their experiences, however, if conditions are just right. He says in *The Case For and Against Psychic Belief* that he has noticed that "if a small group of intelligent men, not supposed to be impressed by psychical research, get together and such matters are mentioned, and all feel that they are in safe and sane company, usually about half of them begin to relate . . . some incident which happened to him or to some member of his family, or to some friend whom he trusts, and which he thinks odd and extremely puzzling."

This is the experience your author also has. Now that those who meet me are aware that they will get a sympathetic hearing for any startling or curious supernormal problems they may wish to confide, my ear is bent with almost tedious inevitability by at least every third person I encounter.

So actually, dear reader, your own sister, or the man next door, may be enjoying exciting out-of-body excursions night after night, but you will probably never hear of it.

Dr. Hornell Hart, professor of sociology at Florida Southern College, in an attempt to discover just how extensive such unconventional travel might be, submitted a questionnaire to 155 students at Duke University in 1952. Of these students, thirty percent answered *"Yes"* to the following question:

"Have you ever actually seen your physical body from a viewpoint completely outside that body, like standing beside the bed and looking at yourself lying in the bed, or like floating in the air near your body?"

Two other groups, who answered the same question, gave somewhat smaller percentages; but it seems safe to conclude, according to Dr. Hart, that at least twenty percent of college-level young people believe that they have had experiences of this sort. Of those who reported "Yes," at least seventy percent remember more than one such projection of viewpoint.

Psychical researchers (or parapsychologists) are those who take the time to study and investigate phenomena which fall outside the known natural laws, and so are called supernormal. Parapsychologists deal primarily with aspects of the mind which are either overlooked or dismissed by most other disciplines. (Psychiatrists and psychologists in the past have been accused of bitterly resenting the claims that psychic [or psi] phenomena were genuine. This was primarily because if it could be proved irrefutably that paranormal powers of the mind, like telepathy, clairvoyance, precognition, and psychokinesis, actually exist, many previously held theories would become invalid. Now that such proof can be accepted almost without question, these doctors are changing their minds. A poll taken in 1948 by New York City psychiatrist and neurologist, Dr. Russell G. MacRobert, of 2,510 diplomates of the American Board of Psychiatry and Neurology and members of the Association for Research in Nervous and Mental Disease, showed that 68 percent of the responding doctors believed that they should look into the truth and significance of these extrasensory and psychical happenings. Probably the number would be much larger now.)

The history of philosophy shows that there has been what Dr. J. Gaither Pratt refers to as "a continual battle waxing and waning over thousands of pages of unending and seemingly unendable debate, over what place, if any, mind occupies in the universe." Dr. Pratt, formerly of the Duke University Parapsychology Laboratory and now with the University of Virginia, says in his book *Parapsychology: An Insider's View of ESP:* "The revolutionary findings of parapsychology are the facts which cannot be accommodated to any view of the universe which equates all existence with those things that are the proper concern of physics: Mass and energy operating within a space-time frame of reference. The psi facts *require* that we recognize that there is an additional quality in the realm of experience, a quality which is so unexpected from the point of view of accepted physiological principles that it inevitably suggests the presence in man of something beyond the physical aspects of the universe. This unique attribute in living beings we can . . . simply designate as *mind.*"

Since it is the mind which is said to go wandering away from the physical organism in out-of-body experiences, these are considered to be psychical phenomena. Yet even parapsychologists are divided about whether or not to list them as genuine manifestations. It is possible, some say, that they may be nothing more than hallucinations, and so would be within the province of psychology and not parapsychology, having nothing supernormal about them. Yet the absolute similarity of the many independent stories which have been reported, and the volume of such cases, make their value *en masse* almost staggering. The fact also exists that many who believe they are projecting their minds from their bodies return with information they had no way to acquire normally—as Mary Sharpe came back from her flight with the knowledge of Edwin Emeny's appearance. It is things such as this that make many other psychical researchers feel that it is imperative that some accounting be made for out-of-body experiences.

Such eminent men as Professor Hart, Dr. C. J. Ducasse, professor emeritus of philosophy, Brown University, and numerous others, agree with Professor C. D. Broad of Cambridge University, that such out-of-body states "constitute a very interesting and important class of experience." They feel, therefore, that it is necessary to study, investigate, and propound theories which might help us to understand them.

Still, we are compelled to confess that the occasions are so rare when anything remotely resembling actual proof is obtained that a case where evidence is available is welcomed with open arms. Such a one appeared in *Fate*, September, 1963, and it has been followed up with letters to its author and her witnesses.

Carol Hales of Quartz Hills, California, writes that on the evening of May 28, 1961, she saw a vision in the branches of a tall eucalyptus tree in her yard. It was the face of her friend Miss Jaime Palmer, in whose agonized countenance she read a message of dire need.

"I'll help you," Miss Hales promised the image of her friend, and it faded away. Carol then rushed to the telephone to call Jaime Palmer, but there was no answer.

If Jaime could not answer the telephone, she could not answer the doorbell, so a telegram would be useless, as also would be a visit to her house, which was ten miles away. Besides, a bad storm had arisen. A call to the police would probably not be well received by anyone concerned, either, so Miss Hales felt desperate. Lying down on her bed, she turned to prayer for help. Soon a sense of relief broke through her anxiety.

Then, she says, "As I lay on my bed I felt as if I were rising and drifting easily and comfortably from my body, from my room, from my home. I seemed to be drifting in a calm, aware of the wild shriek and the tremendous blow of the wind, yet untouched by it." The storm had quieted by the time she reached the home of her friend. She found herself entering Jaime's bedroom by way of the balcony, and discovered her lying on her bed in an almost unconscious state.

"I knew at once she was desperately ill," Carol writes. "Moving to the bedside I laid my hand upon her forehead. She stirred restlessly and moaned."

Carol knew she had to get help some way. She returned to the balcony and floated over the railing and drifted slowly down to the garden. There, "I recall touching an orange tree and tightening my fingers about a piece of its green foliage," she says.

The next thing she knew she was back in her bed, *and* held in her hand a sprig of bright green leaves from an orange tree. There were no orange trees near her home, so she knew without doubt that what had happened to her had been no dream. She says: "Sure of the action I must take, I telephoned my good friend and physician, Dr. Marion J. Dakin, and told her that I was sure my friend Miss Palmer was very ill and I asked her to help."

Dr. Dakin and her nurse, Mrs. Unetta Morse, went immediately to the Palmer home. They knocked and called loudly, but there was no answer. They tried all the doors. By a stroke of luck someone had forgotten to lock a side door and they entered. Then they found Jaime, desperately ill. She was rushed to Santa Monica Hospital, where immediate surgery was performed by Dr. Earl Boehme with Dr. Dakin in attendance. An exceptionally large gallstone was removed, which, they later told Miss Palmer, was in such a position that it would soon have ruptured the intestinal wall.

Miss Palmer writes as a testimonial: "It is my understanding from both doctors, and the nurses at the hospital, that I would not have lived if I had not had immediate surgery." She added that Carol was instrumental in bringing this about in the manner stated in her article. She recalls that at the onset of her gall bladder attack she had thought, "I don't want to worry Carol, but I may have to have her help."

"If my experience was merely a dream," Miss Hales asks, "then where did I get the foliage from an orange tree? And how did I know of Jaime's desperate need?"

Such spontaneous cases, occurring as they so frequently do during times of crisis, illness, anesthesia, etc., depend entirely on testimony for verification. The scientific investigator would, of course, prefer to have first-hand observations under controlled experimental conditions. So it is of great interest to researchers that certain persons claim to be able to have these experiences at will. They may even on occasion perform under test conditions. Some interesting research with people having this faculty is now being undertaken in Finland, among other places.

Four men, Sylvan Muldoon, Oliver Fox (pseudonym for Hugh Callaway), Dr. J. H. M. Whiteman, and a French writer whose nom de plume is Yram, all have learned to leave their bodies whenever they wish. They have experimented endlessly and have written highly introspective books about their numerous "astral projections," as they call them. (Other terms descriptive of the phenomenon as it varies in specific instances are travelling clairvoyance, ESP projection, self-projection, bilocation, and extrasensory travel. Occult writers almost always use the terms astral or etheric projection or astral travel.)

Such experiences are so subjective, however, that the researcher cannot accept what these people say of their projections as *proof* that their minds were actually away from their bodies. Proof is not easy to come by in the psychic field. Actually, as the reader has probably already observed, neither the parapsychologist nor the occultist is sure exactly what an out-of-body experience is, or how, or why it occurs, or even *if* it will invariably occur under given circumstances.

Thus, a writer on this subject cannot be dogmatic about it. Just about the only thing he can do is to interview persons who say they have had such experiences, procure testimony of witnesses if such exist, classify the information, and compare it with other similar data. He may also quote the conclusions of others who have studied these data carefully.

Such a conclusion will now be quoted. It was reached by Professor Hornell Hart, who says that the hypothesis of extrasensory travel seems to be supported, by reports of spontaneous and experimental cases, with such evidential strength that the likelihood of its actual occurrence seems fairly high. And "the major significance of the hypothesis is so great, with respect to philosophy, religion, and the whole orientation of life—that the need for further rigorous and comprehensive research in the field seems imperative."

It is in an effort to bring together such significant material and to try to evaluate it in a meaningful way that this book is written.

2

Spontaneous
Cases

SPONTANEOUS OUT-OF-BODY EXPERIENCES MAY OCCUR ONLY ONCE in a lifetime, as in the case of Mary Sharpe, or they may come with relative frequency. While sometimes purposeful, they often appear to have no reason whatever. There are on record countless instances where someone believes himself to be floating over forest, hill or stream, or even ocean, in an aimless expedition which, while of interest to the participant, seems to have no actual value or purpose.

Such an incident occurred to Mrs. Hilda D. Williams, who is quoted by Dr. Robert Crookall in *The Study and Practice of Astral Projection* as saying: "One night I went to sleep. My next recollection is of standing in my room; the furniture and other details were quite clear." She walked through her house, outside the front door, and down the road. But at about two hundred yards from the house she wanted to return.

"On turning round," she says, "I saw a shining white cord, two or three inches wide, composed of four or five loosely woven strands, stretching from my body, as far as I could see, back to the house. The next thing I knew, I was standing at the side of my bed and saw my Physical Body. The cord was attached to the head of my Psychical Body and to the center of my Physical Body. I thought, 'I must get in,' slipped into bed, and awoke. I had not been aware of leaving the body but re-entering it felt like slipping the hand into an easy-fitting glove."

Mrs. Williams was sure that her experience was not a dream. Next I give another in which the subject was equally as convinced that she *was* dreaming. But was she? At the very same time she was seen by her mother in a distant place.

A young woman who calls herself Martha Johnson, twenty-six years old, single, and living several hundred miles from home, dreamed on the night of January 26, 1957, that she was particularly angry about something and wished to tell her mother. She began walking, in her dream, eventually going through considerable blackness at what seemed to be a great height. Then all at once she could see a small bright oasis of light down below her and she knew it was her mother's house. She walked into the kitchen. "After I entered," she says in her report to the American Society for Psychical Research, "I leaned up against the dish cupboard with folded arms, a pose I often assume. I looked at my mother, who was bending over something white and doing something with her hands. She did not appear to see me at first, but she finally looked up. I had a pleased feeling, and then, after standing a second more, I turned and walked about four steps." Then Miss Johnson was enveloped in a mist, and at this point she awoke. She looked at her bedside clock and noted the time—2:10 a.m. In a few days she received a letter from her mother stating that while ironing in her kitchen she had seen Martha that same night at the very same time. Her mother was not surprised, for apparently her daughter had visited her in dreams before.

In contrast to the mildly pleasant dream projection, a great crisis may cause an abrupt and painful ejection of the consciousness from the body. Author Ernest Hemingway, as a youth of nineteen, was serving in the armed forces in Italy. About midnight July 8, 1918, he was in a trench near the village of Fossalta handing out chocolate to Italian soldiers when an Austrian mortar shell loaded with scrap metal landed close by. Hemingway was badly wounded in the legs by shrapnel.

By his own account to his friend Guy Hickok, European correspondent for the Brooklyn *Daily Eagle,* he died then.

"I felt my soul or something coming right out of my body, like you'd pull a silk handkerchief out of a pocket by one corner," he said. "It flew around and then came back and went in again and I wasn't dead any more."

Hemingway used this in chapter nine of his novel A *Farewell to Arms,* a fictional treatment of his actual experience written about ten years after the incident. His hero Frederick Henry is in the Italian trenches eating a piece of chocolate and taking a swallow of wine. Then he hears something like a cough and a chugging noise. Then there is a flash, which Henry describes "as when a blast-furnace door is swung open, and a roar that started white and went red and on and on in a rushing wind. I tried to breathe but my breath would not come and I felt myself rush bodily out of myself and out and out and out and all the time bodily in the wind. I went out swiftly, all of myself, and I knew I was dead and that it had all been a mistake to think you just died. Then I floated, and instead of going on I felt myself slide back. I breathed and I was back."

Out-of-body experiences may also be brought on by need or desire. The simple goal of trying to get a glass of water caused Stanley Goldberg of Jamaica, Long Island, to have his one and only outing of this nature. Goldberg is a reader of psychical literature, although at that time he knew only enough about astral projection to be aware that it could happen. Certainly he had never thought it might favor him.

At four o'clock one morning in 1948 Stanley awoke very thirsty. He tried to get out of bed but found himself in a cataleptic state and could not move. Mentally he was quite alert, although startled then to be suddenly in the kitchen trying to reach for a glass to get a drink of water. His hand went right through the door of the cabinet, and he could not grasp a glass.

"Oddly enough," he says, "although it was dark night, the entire room seemed to be in a twilight of silvery-blue radiation."

Stanley walked into the living room and toward the window. He was beginning now to realize what might be going on, and he wanted to savor it to the fullest while he could. But just at that moment he felt a strong pulling sensation at the back of his neck. He was turned around and jerked backwards sharply, right through the wall and into his own room. Then he made a neat three-point landing into his physical body.

Stanley took his initial trip calmly, probably because he knew vaguely the *modus operandi* involved. Consider the plight of an individual who begins to have astral projections rather frequently, but who is not aware that such things ever occur. A man I know has told me in some detail of his serious alarm at this. Because he is a prominent businessman in a large city, this gentleman insists upon remaining anonymous, so we will refer to him as George Jones. He was desperately frightened when he first began to float out of his body while it lay quietly on his bed. Could he have suddenly developed a defective heart or high blood pressure that was giving him highly unusual symptoms? He rushed to his doctor. Electrocardiograms, angiograms and other tests revealed no negative condition. He then visited an ear specialist, because a hissing sound sometimes accompanied his psychic excursions. This medic told him that nothing was wrong with his ears, that he had apparently just acquired the rather eccentric habit of listening to the pounding of his own pulse.

Since he was physically sound, what could be the cause of his alarming condition? George Jones inevitably came to the conclusion that it must be totally hallucinatory in nature and motivated by some mental disorder. Fortunately for his peace of mind, he learned from a friend that there are books describing such strange occurrences, and that other ostensibly sane persons have them. He read these books avidly. His mind then at ease, he learned to make the most of his interesting affliction. He began to use his executive-type logical thinking processes to analyze calmly to his own satisfaction these special talents he had suddenly acquired. He now experiments enthusiastically.

To my friend Joan Cartwright, by way of contrast, once in a lifetime was quite enough, and she has no desire for a repetition of her out-of-body experience. Mrs. Cartwright, of Preston, Lancashire, England, took sodium pentothol in a dentist's office in 1959 and suddenly her mind seemed completely detached from her body. She says, "I couldn't tell you how I got up there but the thinking part of me was up in the air . . . in space. . . . It seemed to be higher than the ceiling." She looked back down and saw herself sitting in the chair; but although she knew what was going on there, she could not actually *see* the dentist filling her tooth.

Joan was particularly impressed with the "enormous feeling of aloneness" she had up there, which was mentally very disturbing. Later she realized all at once that she was back again in the dentist's chair; and since that time she does not recall the episode if she can help it. "The feeling never has left me whenever I think about it," she says. "To tell the truth, it wasn't a very nice experience. I can't say that I enjoyed it."

Just the opposite of this uncomfortable circumstance is one described by the noted psychoanalyst C. G. Jung in *Memories, Dreams, Reflections.* Jung had broken his foot and then had a heart attack. For some time he lingered between life and death, and it was then that he had a series of momentous nightly visions. "Once," he wrote, "it seemed to me that I was high up in space. Far below I saw the globe of earth, bathed in a gloriously blue light. I saw the deep blue sea and the continents. Below my feet lay Ceylon, and in the distance ahead of me the subcontinent of India. My field of vision did not include the whole earth, but its global shape was plainly distinguishable and its outlines shone with a silvery gleam through that wonderful blue light. In many places the globe seemed colored, or spotted dark green like oxydized silver. Far away to the left lay a broad expanse—the reddish-yellow desert of Arabia; it was as though the silver of the earth had there assumed a reddish-gold hue. Then came the Red Sea, and far, far back—as if in the upper left of a map—I could just make out a bit of the Mediterranean. . . ."

Jung later estimated that in order to have been high enough to have so broad a view of the world, he would have had to be a thousand miles up. "The sight of the earth from this height was the most glorious thing I had ever seen," he said.

Of his whole series of episodes Jung wrote: "It is impossible to convey the beauty and intensity of emotion during those visions. They were the most tremendous things I have ever experienced." Although he called them visions, he said of them: "I would never have imagined that any such experience was possible. It was not a product of imagination. The visions and experiences were utterly real; there was nothing subjective about them; they all had a quality of absolute objectivity."

In contrast to Jung's more critical appraisal, Mrs. A. C. Billeter of Belt, Montana, believes in the complete reality of her experience, which brought her a peace of mind she had never before known. She had a heart condition which occasionally rendered her helpless and unable to speak. One night in November, 1949, during such an attack she found herself standing beside her bed looking down at her body there. She felt light and free and went out of the house without even bothering to open the door. She walked through a forest and came upon a clear stream with sandy banks.

"Then," she said, "I felt a slight tugging as if a small, invisible thread held me to that other body. But I did not want to go back and so I crossed the stream." She was aware as she did this that she was not wading in the water, but she felt so fine that she was not worrying about what her actual means of locomotion was. A voice interrupted her reverie. "You have to go back," it said.

"I did not want to," Mrs. Billeter writes in *Fate*, November, 1963, "but the voice insisted, and so I retraced my steps with the thread tugging me toward the other body. I went through the closed door and merged with my flesh body. Then and then only did I feel ill. I labored for breath."

Mrs. Billeter adds, "Since that night I know there is no death but only a severing of spirit from flesh. I am thankful for this experience, for I am no longer terrified by the thought of dying."

A similar instance having inspirational significance which has enriched all the rest of her life, occurred to Julia Phillips Ruopp of Minneapolis, Minnesota, long ago during a thyroid operation. She was suddenly looking down at herself and the doctors and nurses from a short distance over their heads. She heard the anesthetist say, "Doctor, her pulse is going." Then she started through what seemed to be a long, dark passageway, and as she went along she thought calmly, "This must be what they call dying."

Mrs. Ruopp writes in *Guideposts* for October, 1963: "This journey continued uneventfully for some time . . ." but finally she found herself looking into an enormous convex window. "I knew that it was not glass," she says, "for I could easily have stepped through to the other side; at the same time the thought came to me that I must be looking through a window into one bright spot of Heaven. What I saw there made all earthly joys pale into insignificance." She was delighted then to see a merry throng of children singing and frolicking in an apple orchard, and she longed to join them. Then she became aware of a presence of joy, harmony and compassion which was beside her. Her heart yearned to become a part of this beauty; but somehow she could not bring herself to go through the window. "An invisible, tenacious restraint pulled me back each time I leaned forward with that intention," she writes.

After a time she returned to her body; and then during the next twenty-four hours, while she was in a critical condition, "all the meanings of life and death seemed to pass before my inner eyes," she says.

Mrs. Ruopp recovered, and for the thirty years since then she has had a busy and useful life as the wife of a minister and a mother. But she has never forgotten her glimpse of Heaven and the very real and inspiring lessons she learned from the "flash revelation about the meaning of life itself."

Cases of this sort, while undoubtedly of great psychological value to the participant, are classified as hallucinations by a fictitious parapsychologist whom I have chosen to be our Devil's Advocate. Because nothing of evidential value occurred, he will say. Yet when we give him some cases where the projector returns with information, he will declare that the same data could probably have been received by some form of extrasensory perception, and the experience is therefore not necessarily an out-of-body one.

This is exactly what he would say about the testimony of Mary Stuart Albrecht of New York City. Mrs. Albrecht is absolutely sure that she has projected her mind away from her body on three different occasions, and that she has returned with information which was evidential because she had no normal means of acquiring it. One night in 1943 Mrs. Albrecht closed her eyes in her New York apartment and immediately found herself in the large family home in Olney, Illinois, where her two ancient aunts lived. Completely conscious and aware that she was not dreaming, Mrs. Albrecht wandered through the lovely old house.

When she reached the room in which her aunts slept together in one bed, she was suddenly filled with the greatest joy. "It was an ecstasy I had never felt before," she says; and she knew without any doubt that one of the figures in the bed was dead instead of sleeping, and was in a rapturous state.

The next morning Mrs. Albrecht told her daughter Nina, a commercial artist, that she was sure her Aunt Betty had died in her sleep early the night before. Then she related all the events of her experience. Soon a telegram arrived with the news of Aunt Betty's death; and later letters confirmed all the details just as she had seen them.

Eileen J. Garrett, president of the Parapsychology Foundation and a medium of the highest repute, has had many spontaneous occurrences of this nature during which she has travelled clairvoyantly, acquiring information.

During World War II Mrs. Garrett was particularly interested in the welfare of an English woman who had married a Breton named Fiattre and was living in the little French village of St. Jacut. One night Mrs. Garrett, in America, visited Brigit Fiattre in France, starting with a dream and ending up with a feeling of actual physical presence at the foreign spot. She had never been to St. Jacut, but soon located the house of her friend, rather close to the cliffs. Around the house and near the beach there was a weird and menacing collection of individuals who looked decidedly Mongolian, and spoke in a rough staccato rather like Chinese. Mrs. Garrett completed her secret nocturnal visit to her friend's home and then awakened, greatly curious about why these Orientals were in France.

In 1947 she visited Brigit Fiattre in person and told her of her dream, particularly mentioning the strange men she had seen. "You can imagine my astonishment," she says, "when she revealed to me that the German occupation forces had brought with them a number of Mongolian laborers who were engaged around the cliffs in building blockhouses and high walls." They were an odd group who had fallen into the hands of the Germans and were being used as labor units in various areas of France. Mrs. Garrett says that conditions inside the house had also been as she had seen them during her nocturnal sojourn.

On another occasion during the war period Eileen Garrett learned from her daughter "Babs" that her husband had not been heard from for some time. A curtain of secrecy had fallen over his unit, and she was afraid he might have been sent into action.

That night Mrs. Garrett found herself astrally searching for her son-in-law in Skye, an island in the Hebrides. She says, "I inquired for the French unit and was told that it was further away in the Orkney Islands." She had to learn exactly where the Orkneys were in reference to her position, and then she went right across the tip of Scotland, and there the Orkneys were, and there the French outfit was also.

The next day Mrs. Garrett wrote a letter of reassurance that her daughter's husband was not abroad or in any danger. It was not long afterwards that security bans were lifted and Babs received official notification that her husband was training in the Orkneys.

A case of travelling clairvoyance which occurred during an operation was related by Dr. O., a chief surgeon at Lenox Hill Hospital in New York City, to his colleague, Dr. Russell MacRobert, who published it in *The Maple Leaf*. The patient for a brief but painful ear operation was a clergyman known to the surgeon as an especially sensitive person, so the anesthetist had been instructed to keep him deeply unconscious.

When everything, patient included, was prepared for the operation, Dr. O. asked the nurse for a special instrument. He was told that it had not been sterilized. Much annoyed, he cussed roundly, as surgeons are apt to do, pulled off his sterile gloves and gown and stomped out of the room and down the hall to where he had left an instrument bag. He brought back the tool he wanted, gave it to the nurse to be sterilized, and got back into fresh gown and gloves. Then he proceeded with the operation, which went well.

However, the patient was so profoundly comatose that for a time it looked as though he might not recover from the anesthesia. When he did come to, he reported that all during the surgery he was outside his body but in full possession of his senses and able to move about. He correctly described actions and unusual remarks that had been made. Also, he had left the operating room with the surgeon, and had gone with him down the hall when he procured the instrument from his bag. He told where the nurses had stood at certain times during the operation. He related the conversations that he had overheard. And he jokingly chided Dr. O. for having used language improper in the presence of a clergyman. The chagrin and astonishment of the doctors and nurses at his story were extreme. After this, Dr. O. probably looks nervously over his shoulder whenever he gets mad enough to cuss during an operation.

Now, for every ten cases where the individual remembers what happened during his astral projection, there is one in which he does not. Then how do we know he was having one? Because somebody saw him.

An incident of this kind occurred when Delbert Savage of Au Sable Forks, New York, was in the Navy serving in the Caroline Islands in 1944. One afternoon he was sitting on his bunk listening to his shipmates talking. He had been there about half an hour, he tells me, when "I was dumbfounded to find my wife suddenly sitting right beside me. I was very happy to see her, and momentarily it flashed through my mind to wonder how she had gotten on board the ship all those thousand miles from home. Of course, the first thing I did was to reach for her, but as I did this she vanished." Savage says it was some time before he could gather his wits about him. He was so pale that one of his shipmates asked him if he was ill. He never told anyone on board the ship about the experience; and no one ever twitted him about his visitor, so he knows that he was the only one to see her. When Savage later asked his wife about the instance, he learned that she had not been aware of her sea voyage. But she wasn't surprised, because she thought of her husband constantly.

Delbert Savage suspects that he may have hallucinated an apparition out of his deep longing for his wife. But then again, perhaps she was with him briefly. No one can say for sure she wasn't.

Certainly there was no doubt in the mind of Vera Christopher of Holdenville, Oklahoma, that she actually saw her mother. Mrs. Christopher said in *Fate*, February, 1964, that, almost completely paralyzed from a stroke, her mother, Mrs. Almae Shelden, had required constant care, day and night, for several months. Mrs. Christopher and her sister Bonnie E. Harding took turns staying with her at night, resting in snatches on a cot in her room. On the night of January 20, 1963, Vera lay resting but awake when suddenly she was amazed to see her mother moving lightly and happily around the room. She walked over to her daughter's cot and smiled at her.

Vera sat up and said, "Why, Mom, you're walking." But then she glanced toward her mother's bed and saw her figure still there sleeping. Vera's eyes returned to the woman standing in front of her. Although the room was lighted only dimly, she could see that it was clearly her mother, who then walked back to the bed, became horizontal over the wasted sleeping body, and faded or merged into it.

Vera told her sister Bonnie of this the first thing the next morning; but they were never able to learn if their mother had been aware that her spirit had been momentarily free, for she was never able to speak coherently after that time.

Bonnie Harding, who lives in Placerville, California, writes me that she, herself, has had partial astral projections for years. They are very pleasant, but they have not overawed her too much because they never have come up to any standards of evidence.

"For some strange reason," she says, "I could never get myself upright—always stayed horizontal." However, she could look down at her own body on the bed, and this is, to many, a criterion of a genuine manifestation.

Mrs. Harding travelled, rather aimlessly it is true, and could see trees and streets and oceans, but there was still nothing she considers of any great value. Having read the books written by Oliver Fox and Sylvan Muldoon, she is completely unimpressed by her own wayfaring as compared with their much more spectacular revelations.

3

Habitual Travellers

PEOPLE WHO HAVE FREQUENT ASTRAL PROJECTIONS USUALLY BE-
gin with a spontaneous event similar to those just related, and
then learn to repeat it at will.

Oliver Fox tells in his book *Astral Projection* of his first out-
of-body experience—and it all came out of a dream. In the
spring of 1902 when he was sixteen years old, he dreamed one
night that he was standing on the pavement outside his home,
and the magic of the early morning sunshine made the scene
unusually beautiful. He looked at the paving stones of the
street and they were reversed, running lengthwise to the curb.
He wondered about this. "Then," he says, "the solution flashed
upon me: though this glorious summer morning seemed as
real as real could be, I was dreaming!"

With the realization of this fact, the quality of the dream
changed in a manner very difficult to convey, he says, to one
who has not undergone anything similar. "Instantly the vividness of life increased a hundredfold. Never had sea and sky
and trees shone with such glamorous beauty; even the commonplace houses seemed alive and mystically beautiful. Never had
I felt so absolutely well, so clear-brained, so divinely powerful,
so inexpressibly *free!* The sensation was exquisite beyond words;
but it lasted only a few moments, and I awoke."

Sylvan Muldoon's projecting also began when he was very
young, when he had what was probably the most harrowing

youthful adventure since Jack climbed the Beanstalk. One night when he was twelve years old he awoke in a powerless condition, unable even to see or hear. Yet he was conscious and he was somewhere, he just couldn't think where. The rigid state began to relax and he felt himself to be floating; then his body began vibrating at a great rate of speed. He seemed to be zigzagging about and he felt a strong pressure on the back of his head. At first he thought he was having some queer nightmare in total darkness. Gradually his sight and hearing were restored, and then he realized that he was floating in the air high over his bed.

In a short time he was uprighted, and then he looked back down and saw his body. There were two of him! One in the air and one on the bed! The boy was beginning to think himself insane. Of course, he ran to his mother, passing right through the door as he went. But mother could not hear him, nor feel him shaking her. He tried everyone else in the house with the same results. Then, quite logically, he started to cry.

Luckily, the force at the back of his neck finally pulled him back toward his physical body. His astral body assumed a horizontal position directly over his bed, it was slowly lowered, and then dropped quickly, coinciding with its physical counterpart once more. He then felt a penetrating pain as if he had been split open from head to foot.

Naturally this child had no idea what had happened to him, but he was sure he didn't like it. Many years elapsed before he ever came upon any literature on the subject and learned that the same thing also befell others; but in the meantime he had frequent projections, increasingly less alarming to him as they became more commonplace.

When he began to read psychic and occult literature, he discovered the immense amount of factual material which existed and the antiquity of the doctrine. He relates in *The Phenomena of Astral Projection*: "I found that in ancient Egypt, in China, Tibet, India and throughout the Orient generally, this idea was almost universally accepted, and had been for centuries past. I found that primitive peoples of our own day held similar views, and that much actual experimental work had been undertaken by scientific psychic investigators, in their attempts to secure adequate evidence."

It was when reading Hereward Carrington's book *Modern Psychical Phenomena* that Muldoon finally realized the character and importance of his own experiences, and at the same time how relatively little was generally known concerning such things. He contacted Carrington and told him that his adventures were more numerous and more fascinating than any previously published. The outgrowth of their correspondence about this was several jointly written books which have been a source of curiosity and enlightenment to many.

Another first encounter with our subject matter was reported graphically by British novelist William Gerhardi, who says, "All readers who have not themselves experienced astral projection are sure to put it down to a dream, or attribute it to some form of mental disorder. But nobody who has experienced it himself would for a moment admit that any such confusion was possible."

Gerhardi was being interviewed by a reporter from the London *Sunday Express* and he was admitting publicly an event with which many persons are totally unfamiliar. He therefore tried to describe his sensations carefully and exactly. "It has no resemblance to dreaming," he said. "If the whole world united in telling me it was a dream I would remain unconvinced." Gerhardi was positive it was not a dream because he had been dreaming before it happened and awoke with a start. He stretched out his hand to press the switch of the lamp on the book-shelf over his bed and instead found himself grasping the void, for he was suspended precariously in mid-air, on a level with the bookcase.

Except for the light of the electric stove, the room was in darkness, but, he said, "all around me was a milky pellucid light, like steam. I was that moment fully awake, and so fully conscious that I could not doubt my senses, astonished as I have never been before, amazed to the point of proud exhilaration."

He seemed to be supported as if by a steel arm which held him rigid, yet this was ludicrous, for he actually felt light as a feather. After his first moment of delighted astonishment, Gerhardi became apprehensive. This caused a change in his condition—the force holding him up seemed to grow suddenly energetic. He was swiftly pushed about, placed on his feet, thrust forward, and then turned around.

"And turning, I became aware for the first time of a strange appendage," he said. "At the back of me was a coil of light, like a luminous garden hose resembling the strong broad ray of dusty light at the back of a dark cinema projecting on the screen in front. To my utter astonishment, that broad cable of light at the back of me illumined the face on the pillow that I recognized as my very own, as if attached to the brow of the sleeper.

"It was myself, not dead, but breathing peacefully, my mouth slightly open. My cheeks were flushed, my face, lying sideways and deeply sunk into the pillow, was pathetic and touching in its vacant innocence of expression; and here was I, outside it, watching it with a thrill of joy and fear."

As he began to move about, it was like wading through an unsteady sea. "I staggered uncertainly to the door," he said. "I felt the handle, but to my discomfiture I could not turn it; there was no grip in my hand; it seemed unreal."

"Now, how will I get out?" he thought, for it seemed that someone had taken all the strength out of his wrist. At that moment he was pushed forward, the door passed through him, or he through the door, with a marked absence of resistance after wading through the heavy space.

"Avidly," he says, "I went from room to room, trying to collect what proof I could. I was alone in the flat, which was in darkness except for the murky light which seemed to emanate from my own body." His consciousness grew bright and again dim, bright and dim; but at one of his more lucid moments he realized that there was probably not much time at his disposal for collecting evidence which would convince him later of the reality of his experience. He says:

"I could not hold anything in my hand or displace the lightest of objects, so all I could do was to note carefully the position of things; which curtains were open or drawn, the time by the clock in the dining room; and things of that sort. Which all proved correct when I checked them later."

Suddenly the strange power began to play pranks with him and he was pushed up like a half-filled balloon. Out he flew through the front door and then he hovered outside in the air. A feeling of extraordinary lightness of heart came over him. He knew that he could now transport himself at will had he chosen to do so, but caution intervened, a fear that something might happen to sever the silver cord which attached him to the body sleeping on the bed.

"No, not today," he decided. "Enough for the first time. Let me get back." And so he flew back to his bed. Then his consciousness became dimmed, and suddenly, with a jerk, he was back in his body and opening his eyes.

Gerhardi related one more thing which adds to our overall picture: as he had travelled about he had caught a glimpse of himself in the bathroom mirror. "I looked to be my own double, and I was dressed exactly as I had gone to bed," he said. "The only difference was a lack of weight and substance about this body."

On Gerhardi's second venturing out of his body, as reported by Robert Crookall in *The Study and Practice of Astral Projection*, he met a friend named Bonzo, and they chatted about various things. Then they went together to Bonzo's house, and they looked together at Bonzo's body lying on the bed.

"The man on the bed was not breathing," Gerhardi says. "The Bonzo at my side, who looked at his double with an air of fastidious, almost quizzical dismay, was the living Bonzo. . . ."

When Gerhardi came back to his physical body from this visit with Bonzo, he called his friend's home immediately. And he learned that Bonzo had taken an anesthetic in order to have a broken wrist bone re-set, and he had not come out from under it. His friend was really dead.

These exploits all sound unrealistic enough to have been concocted by romanticizing novelists; but they are confirmed by the observations of other habitual exteriorizers. Yram is nothing if not calm and cool and carefully observant; in fact, his book is entitled *Practical Astral Projection:*

"You leave your body," he says, "with greater ease than taking off a suit of clothes and you wonder why this faculty is not more widespread. And you are certain that you are alive and awake and that what is happening is not hallucination or suggestion."

J. H. M. Whiteman, author of *The Mystical Life*, adds to this that when one travels out to the "higher levels" the breathing seems to stop, and the respose of the physical body is so complete that, to an onlooker, the soul might be supposed to have peacefully passed away.

"I deduce that this is so," he says, "partly because that is how the physical body appears to me at the time, and partly because on one occasion . . . my wife became alarmed at the deathlike stillness of my physical body, and by touching it caused me to return."

Sometimes there are sensations of floating, whirling or zig-zagging as one exteriorizes. One may see lights, images, figures, and hear sounds of various kinds, from inarticulate noises to beautiful music. Some astral travellers can make contact with physical objects such as door knobs; some cannot. A slight dizziness is often noticed at the beginning of their experience. Sometimes there is a brief black-out. The idea of going down a tunnel is fairly common.

"I close my eyes and have a feeling of going over backwards, and I find myself going down a long dim tunnel," is the way one individual described it. Someone else said he "had the extraordinary sensation of being drawn out horizontally through a small hole in the center of the skull."

Yram says, "The final sensation in which all others culminate is that of 'coming out' of something, of leaving a narrow, tight place. . . . Immediately on becoming free a feeling of well-being flows through us; we seem to breathe with greater ease; the consciousness has a feeling of unaccustomed freedom. . . .'"

Whiteman, and others, have found it possible to originate astral flight from a vision. Whiteman reports that he was once lying quietly on his bed fully awake when he perceived an opening with a circular boundary through which he was presented a scene in bright sunlight and vivid colors. It appeared to be a park with many people walking peacefully about.

"At the same time," he says, "I was aware of the physical body lying on its back in bed, but not altogether as if I were in that body. It was as if I were apart and watching the physical body watching." He conceived a wish to visit the park and immediately found himself proceeding there, although his body remained on the bed. He soon met and mingled with the people in his vision.

Another way to embark on an astral voyage is from a dream, as Oliver Fox did on his first time out. But it has to be an especial type of dream—the kind which was labeled a "lucid dream" by a Dutch doctor named F. van Eeden. The essential difference between a lucid dream and an ordinary dream is that in the former the dreamer is aware that he is asleep. He can direct his attention at will and attempt various experiments.

One night in January, 1898, van Eeden dreamed that he was lying face downward in his garden outside the window of his study. Meanwhile he knew quite well that he was in fact asleep and lying on his back in his bedroom. He resolved to try to wake up slowly and carefully and to note the transition from the dream experience of lying on his chest to the reality of lying on his back. He describes it as "like the feeling of slipping from one body into another." He remarks that this leads almost inevitably to the notion of having two bodies.

According to Oliver Fox, learning to have such lucid dreams is the first step to developing astral projection, if, after reading of all his misadventures and misgivings one should still have the temerity to wish to acquire such powers. His other technique, "The Way of Self-Induced Trance," sounds even more difficult, if possible, for in it the experimenter must learn to send the *body* to sleep while the *mind* is kept awake.

All these gentlemen agree that it is also possible for the spirit to leave the body during a drowsy, detached state; and Muldoon recommends deprivation as a successful technique. He says that if one becomes obsessed by a certain desire before going to sleep, he may leave his body while trying to satisfy it. That is what happened to Stanley Goldberg spontaneously, remember? He awoke thirsty and tried to get a drink.

But it isn't always this easy. Yram says that one day, in order to leave his body, he saw himself stretched out face down on a table, gripping and pulling at the edge. "Another time," he says, "I found myself in bed, my head where my feet should have been; and I was moving in a jerky manner which was, then, necessary in order to obtain the desired results. On still another occasion I had the sensation of wrapping myself round the bedpost in order to leave my recalcitrant body."

And once again, Yram speaking, "my astral body was shot out violently like a shell from a gun. I was thrown, face downwards, with my arms stretched out, so realistically that I thought that I had really been thrown from my bed to the floor. There was nothing to give cause for worry. I was well out of my body. . . ."

Oh, no, not a thing to worry about. Not a single little old thing. And returning to the launching pad doesn't seem to be much easier. Muldoon tells us that once he was dreaming he was in a room where "there was but one small hole in the center of the ceiling through which I could see light. . . . It seemed that I stood there for some time when suddenly I wondered if I could not fly through it. I began to rise in the air but as I was passing through the hole I became caught fast in it. . . . At this point I began to awaken and realize what was taking place . . . the position of the astral body corresponded with the position it held in the dream. I was just half-way through the ceiling of the room when I became conscious."

Muldoon was quite awake, he was no longer dreaming, and he was stuck in the ceiling. What did he do now to get out of the awkward situation? He leaves us up in the air, too, for he does not say. But he probably followed one of his usual procedures. Sometimes he could just think himself back into his body and he was there. Or he might have done it the hard way and landed with a bump and a jerk as Gerhardi did.

"When returning to the body," Muldoon says, "the greater the speed and the greater the distance, the more forceful will be the jolt. Velocity and distance combined produce the maximum repercussion; but speed is the more important of the two; for even at a distance of separation of only one foot, if the return to the physical is with intense velocity, the physical will undergo a violent shock."

Muldoon somehow does not feel that this is harmful, and asks the beginner not to be discouraged when such things happen.

One woman described her feelings on her return thus: "I felt my body absorbing me . . . like a sheet of blotting paper, or as a sponge absorbs water."

According to George Jones, "Sometimes when you are exteriorized the thing that will pull you back is a feeling of discomfort in the body. You may not be aware of this until you later find an arm numb or your throat too dry, and then you say, 'Oh, yes, that's what caused me to return.'" Jones has left his body for periods of from twenty minutes to four hours. And he frankly, and unoptimistically, is afraid that some day he may not be able to get back.

Alarm or fear can draw the double back into the body with brutal suddenness, and this is a decidedly uncomfortable sensation, we are told. Muldoon says, "Sounds and emotions will 'shoot' the phantom back into coincidence more quickly than any other opposing factor—often with lightning-like speed. When such takes place, shock is always felt in the physical body—sometimes accompanied by pain; or as I have termed it, a 'split-in-two' feeling."

All these complications incident to experimentation in astral projection would frighten most of us out of our wits, if not out of our bodies; but Muldoon still insists he has *usually* had good results. And Whiteman writes: "In no separation granted to me has there been the slightest compulsion, violence, or rigidity, but exactly the reverse. I believe one may go even further than this, and say that, however much we may be mentally strained, depressed, or caught up in conflict at any time, if for a few moments we are taken freely, by separation, above the levels of fantasy-influence, we return with all strain vanished, and with a new zestful outlook on our physical life. I consider it an infallible test of the healthful and true character of separation that we should return healed and spiritually invigorated for the leading of a better life in this world." Whiteman insists that those who have bad experiences just don't understand and practice correct techniques.

As I begin to get the picture, it would seem that forcing yourself out of your body is dangerous, but if it occurs smoothly and easily it is all right. It must be done by persons who are definitely not neurotic (if you can prove that you're not), and under the most favorable conditions of complete relaxation. Goals must be right and there must be no pressures, and no urgent desires or needs which you are hoping to satisfy. If you have spontaneous astral projections, accept them gratefully as an opportunity to understand other phases of life than those to which you are normally exposed; but for most people it is not wise to seek them. You wouldn't want to make your out-of-body promenading a permanent arrangement.

Muriel Hankey, in her book entitled *J. Hewat McKenzie*, maintains that excess in psychic practice is as dangerous as immoderate indulgence of any appetite; and so the careless or over-indulgent investigator is warned away from experimentation. "But above all," she says, "I would draw attention . . . to the questionable ethics of entering deliberately into these experiences without sanction." She feels it particularly improper to sneak invisibly into the house or room of another and spy upon him, even in the ostensible interests of scientific proof of the experiment.

Oliver Fox has plenty of admonitions, too. He says, "We are dealing with what is essentially a mental exercise or process, and it is easily conceivable that an ill-balanced mind, lacking in self-control, might become temporarily or even permanently deranged."

The possible dangers that Fox foresees are:

1. Heart failure or insanity arising from shock
2. Premature burial
3. Temporary derangement
4. Cerebral haemorrhage
5. Severance of the cord, which means death
6. Repercussion effects upon the physical vehicle caused by injuries to the astral body
7. Obsession

Even though he warns of such appalling possible dangers, Fox would not try to dissuade any earnest investigator with a passion for truth. "Very likely these experiments are no more dangerous than motoring," he says, "but I must confess that I do not really understand what I have been doing. It is easy to say, 'The Soul leaves the body and returns to it'; but this riddle of projection—of what actually happens—is in truth a most profound subject and hedged around with many subtle problems."

Lest we think the dangers outweigh the blessings of this curious phenomenon we are studying, Muldoon has words of assurance. He maintains that if the possibilities suggested by the evidence he offers were accepted by scientists and investigated, "whole new vistas would be opened up; the possibility of survival, the actuality of some sort of spiritual body, the ability to live and think outside the human brain—and heaven knows what else besides."

4

The Astral
Body

NOW, UNLESS ALL THESE PEOPLE WE HAVE BEEN LISTENING TO, and the thousands more who have reported such events, have all been out of their minds as well as out of their bodies, there *must* be more to such experiences than meets the normal eye. Let us delve further into the subject in an attempt to probe the possibilities of Muldoon's strong statement about the importance of this little-known power.

In the first place, if there is something which leaves the body and goes flitting about, what is it? What exactly do others see when they claim to identify someone who is having an astral projection?

Starting from the known as we attempt to reach the unknown—it is a recognized fact that a portion of the physical body which has been removed surgically leaves behind a phantom which still seems to retain feeling. The sense of the wholeness of a missing arm or leg is so real that even if the individual's attention is distracted, he still feels the sensation that the missing part would have felt had it been there. This is medically accepted as the "phantom limb syndrome."

Doctors have a variety of explanations for this, depending upon their own particular fields of study. In *The Painful Phantom*, psychiatrist Lawrence C. Kolb lists a few of these. "The occurrence of the phantom phenomenon," he says, "is best explained as the patient's enduring concept of his total

45

body image after the loss of a part through amputation." Over the period of time since his infancy, by means of multiple postural, tactile, and optic perceptions reaching the cerebral cortex, the individual comes increasingly into his awareness of parts of his body. This sets up a pattern which losing the limb does not change.

Some doctors are inclined more to what they call the peripheral theory, which holds that pain results from some persisting stimulus which occurs at the stump of the severed nerves to the lost appendage . . . mechanical or chemical irritations are considered to set up a bombardment of painful sensory impressions perceived and complained of by the patient. However, "It is common knowledge," Dr. Kolb says, "that repeated surgical treatment of the stump and peripheral nerves . . . is ineffective in relieving the phantom of pain in the majority of patients who· come with this complaint." Some patients undergo continuous treatment of every kind for many years and are never relieved of pain in the phantom limb. Fortunately, in the majority of cases in which feeling remains in the "sensory ghost," no pain at all is felt.

Psychologists use the existence of the phantom to demonstrate the "Gestalt" theory, that is, the continuing psychologic tendency to perceive objects as wholes or as complete.

For the psychiatrist, Dr. Kolb says, "The phantom has often represented a wish-fulfilling hallucination which is motivated as a denial of the loss of the part and the painful affect associated with that loss."

(Speaking of wish-fulfilling, an extremely interesting fact observed by doctors is that patients who require amputations often have had a close and significant emotional attachment to another amputee in the past.)

But what has all this to do with us? Only that some clairvoyants claim that they can *see* phantom limbs. Frau Fredericka Hauffe, a German medium who was studied and observed for years by her medical adviser, Dr. Justinus Kerner (who published a book about her in 1829 entitled *The Seeress* of *Prevorst*), declared that when she met a person with an amputation she could see the missing limb joined to the body in a "fluidic form."

One of the abilities George Jones claims to have discovered is similar to this. While lying on his bed awake and completely relaxed, with his arms and legs immobile, he can by an effort of will lift and move what appear to him to be filmy replicas of his physical limbs, raising and lowering them at his mental commands. He can clasp these spectral hands over his chest while his physical hands are lying at his sides. If he "takes will out of them," as he expresses it, they do not fall quickly to his side, but float back gently to coincide with their normal position. These limbs are transparent but outlined in light.

If actual ghostly duplicates of parts of the body which have been removed still remain, then this might account for the feeling in phantom limbs. George Jones does not speak of having felt any sensation in his astral hands; however, if he had thought about it perhaps he could have felt it.

At one time during the 1930's a rare opportunity presented itself for four highly mediumistic non-professional women and their husbands to spend a period of several weeks investigating psychical phenomena. What they saw is very similar to what Jones reports—and then some.

Betty White, wife of the then well-known American author Stewart Edward White, had developed a strange form of mediumship. While blindfolded and lying quietly on her couch she could "astrally" visit "spirit worlds" and converse with deceased "Invisibles," as she called them. They would give her information about conditions of life after death, and would frequently show her fabulous views of what they were discussing. While Betty was having these projections, her husband sat beside her and wrote down everything she said. In this way a great deal of philosophy of a spiritistic nature was received, which was later published in several books.

The other three women with mediumistic talent were Margaret Cameron, who was another well-known author of that period, a Mrs. Gaines, and Joan, of "Darby and Joan," pseudonyms an Eastern businessman and his wife used in writing a book called *Our Unseen Guest*.

These people were all by temperament and training practical and hardheaded, White assures us, and were known to each other to be of unquestioned integrity. While perhaps not as critical as a group of today's parapsychologists would be, they were nonetheless aware of the need for careful observation and documentation of events.

The Whites had left their California home for an extended visit in the East, and during this period they found time for a series of meetings with these other people. The opportunity to observe four strong non-professional mediums working together under controlled conditions is something for which most psychical researchers would give up a sabbatical year abroad—but let's face it, it is as rare as a visit from Halley's Comet.

White's account of the meetings appeared in *The Betty Book*, in which he writes that when Betty and Joan were heavily and thoroughly blindfolded and put into trance, alleged spirit entities spoke through them. They stated that their goal for the sittings was to prove by actual physical demonstration the existence of what they called the "Beta body."

One night Joan, who was blindfolded and in trance, suddenly called out, "Pinch it! Feel the cold stratum." This cold stratum was readily distinguishable, extending some inches above the floor, like a wintry draught in an old-fashioned house. But it had not been apparent five minutes before and ceased to be apparent five minutes afterwards; and its upper limits were sharply defined. When Joan told them to pinch *her* out there in the cold stratum, it was because she was supposed to be outside her physical body and located in the cold spot. They pinched various areas of it and the blindfolded Joan responded by flinching and wincing as if pinched in the corresponding areas of her own physical body.

On a later occasion the communicant stated: "What we are trying to do is to get her [the medium] to allow the Beta to go out at each of her fingers so you can see the emanations. I think you can see it now if you squinch your eyes."

"We squinched our eyes," White writes, and "saw a faint smoke-like emanation from the ends of the fingers. This increased in density so that shortly everyone in the room could see it plainly with the eyes normal. It was a fine bluish smoke, much like cigarette smoke, but with apparently a slight phosphorescent tinge. The ordinary electric lights were on in the room. This and the succeeding phenomena were seen by everybody, and in most cases from several angles; at distances of from six to eight feet to a close examination within a few inches. After everybody had determined this, a forearm began to form parallel to and about five or six inches above Joan's physical forearm. . . . For perhaps three or four seconds the wrist and hand were also visible to some of us. All present, however, saw the forearm, which lasted for perhaps two minutes or so."

Because supernormal physical manifestations are supposed to be more successful in the dark, they later turned out all light but a darkroom red globe. Then, "At length we were instructed to look at Joan's knees. The effect observed was of voluminous tenuous clouds of rising vapor or smoke. This was not seen at all by Darby, and in varying degrees by the others. Gaines and I apparently got it the strongest. It was as indubitable and physical in appearance as was the smoke of the first experiment, to those who saw it. At the conclusion of the experiment [the communicating entity] said that different people's eyes reacted differently to different colors of light. That, for example, Darby was evidently blind to these emanations in red light. It was somewhat analogous to color-blindness."

Later in a purple light Joan stood up and then slowly her body became indistinct in outline as a lucent fog came in front of it. "This also showed abundantly above her head," White writes. "It spread until practically the whole area surrounding her was filled with it. . . . The entire figure of the body following the outline of the right side, including head and forearm, now formed. . . . Cass, Darby and I remarked at the same instant that the face was slightly in profile. The figure was constant, but the profile was out and in; that is to say, it appeared and disappeared momently. [The entity] instructed someone to 'pinch her.' I pinched this second body at various points, and got quick and strong reactions from Joan's physical body (about eighteen inches distant) from corresponding points—knee, arm, shoulder, head."

Phoebe Payne Bendit, a clairvoyant of unusual ability, possesses a critical mind and considerable powers of detachment. Her husband, Dr. Laurence J. Bendit, a practicing psychiatrist formerly assistant physician at Tavistock Clinic, London, is an analyst of the school of Jung. He is sympathetic, shrewd, and extremely perceptive, and this also helps his wife to keep her special faculty in far greater control than the majority of psychically gifted people. It is because of her known objectivity that researchers are inclined to give consideration to her opinions and observations about her psychic powers, in the same way that they do to Eileen Garrett's.

In their book *The Psychic Sense* the Bendits state that a psychic double of the physical body exists consisting of energy-matter of various densities. They say: "The dense layers are almost visible to the eye, and a very slight extension of normal vision is needed to see it. For instance, if, in a dim light, we touch the tips of the fingers together and then separate the hands it is frequently possible to see streamers of faint greyish mist emanating from the finger-tips. . . ."

A more elaborate technique on which some experimental work was done was to place the hands in a beam of ultra-violet rays passed through special filters, so that the amount of ordinary light was almost nil. By this means many people have been enabled to see the rays more clearly and easily than usual.

Now what all these bits and pieces of semi-transparent bodies add up to is an astral or etheric body—or Beta, if you will, or subtle body, or even the spiritual body which St. Paul insisted resides in each of us. It remains neatly in place in most of us, synchronized with the physical body so that no problems arise. But, if Muldoon is correct, it may leave the body at night during sleep to "recharge its batteries," so to speak. And under some conditions, at times of crisis, trance, coma, epilepsy or under the influence of anesthetics or such, it may be spontaneously ejected. When this occurs, it has these fantastic out-of-body flights we have been discussing.

At death it is supposed to flit merrily away and survive while the physical body perishes. In *The Way of Life* by Arthur Findlay an alleged spirit entity says: "I have a body which is a duplicate of what I had on earth, the same hands, legs and feet, and they move the same as yours do. This etheric body I had on earth interpenetrated the physical body. The etheric is the real body and an exact duplicate of our earth body. At death we just emerge from our flesh covering and continue our life in the etheric world, functioning by means of the etheric body just as we functioned on earth in the physical body. . . ."

Muldoon points out that the astral shape is normally "invisible, intangible, impalpable to the senses, and hence cannot be discovered upon the operating table!" What a shame. If surgeons could remove the astral body and examine it at their leisure with microscopes and tweezers, they might find the answers to many of their most pressing medical problems. George Jones insists, and not without some basis, that if doctors were aware of what he knows about the existence of an astral body it would change the practice of medicine altogether.

But how is there room for a subtle body within what appears to be a tightly meshed solid physical body? That is easy for Muldoon to account for:

"Take an ordinary glass tumbler, for instance. Fill it with round lead bullets, a quarter of an inch in diameter. When these reach the top of the glass, it is said to be 'full.' But it is quite possible to pour in a considerable quantity of buckshot, which filters into the intervening spaces, without making the glass any 'fuller.' After this, sand may be added, with like result. Finally water may be poured in, before the glass may be said to be really 'full.'

"What all this amounts to is really this: That between all particles of matter there is room for still smaller particles, which fill the spaces between them. So far as we can see, this is true of everything, down to the atoms themselves."

Certainly Muldoon's analogy of the glass tumbler would not have held water a few years back, when the body was still thought to be composed entirely of "too too solid flesh." But matter is not considered to be dense and substantial any more. Any atomic physicist will assure you that all matter, the physical body included, is full of holes. Modern physics has informed us that the distances or spaces between the neutrons and protons within an atom are relatively enormous. Can we then insist that some as yet unidentified substance imperceptible to our normal senses might *not* be filling up this space?

Just because we can't see a thing is no sign it isn't there. As C. W. Leadbeater, the Theosophist, says in *Man, Visible and Invisible*, "It is one of the commonest of our mistakes to consider that the limit of our power of perception is also the limit of all that there is to perceive." Our senses are designed only to give us information about certain areas of the world in which we live. Our eyes, for instance, are sensitive only to radiations within a narrow band of wave lengths. As Rolf Schaffranke of the Saturn V moon rocket program in Huntsville, Alabama, says in *Fate*, June, 1964: "It has been said that if we could change the frequency-sensitivity of our eyes to ultraviolet or X-ray wave lengths we would discover the most amazing things about us." Photographic film that has been made sensitive to infra-red rays can photograph objects which are invisible to the human eye, and this has been used occasionally in recent years to take pictures of various unseen psychical phenomena.

But this astral body we are hypothesizing is not purported just to fill in the cracks and crannies of the physical body. It also is supposed to extend outside and all around the body. It is then called an "aura." Many people claim to see this without the slightest difficulty. Some, such as Johannes Greber, D. C., a Catholic priest who devoted the latter years of his life to the investigation of mediumship, think of the aura as surrounding the material body "like a halo" which extends to an equal distance from it at every point, having in consequence the same shape as the body to which it belongs. Others, including the Bendits, assure us that the physical body is penetrated throughout its structure as well as surrounded by the astral body, and it is this "surround" which is seen as the aura.

The Bendits say, in fact, "The double is described as itself a body somewhat larger than the dense physical, so that the latter is like a kernel of heavier matter within the etheric matrix. The appearance it gives of being an aura or surround of the physical body is thus somewhat misleading."

There is great historical tradition for belief in the aura, which, of course, is the "halo" of the saints. The spiritual body which in most cultures is assumed to reside within man and to be immortal, is a body of light. The Egyptian concept of the *ba*, or soul image of man, was his spiritual double which was immortal, and its hieroglyph was a star. Paracelsus, the alchemist, doctor, chemist, and philosopher, said that a half-corporeal body, called the star body, lives beside the body of flesh and is its mirror image. And, of course, occult philosophies accept the aura completely.

As Rolf Schaffranke points out, "It has become the fashion in modern times, even among parapsychologists, to scoff at the human aura, to deny its existence, and to equate it with the imaginative creations of the occultists." But, he believes, "Physics and parapsychology need to get together on this point. More and more scientific investigations are revealing significant findings in this field. Scientists of international stature have been interested and have left the occultists far behind."

Schaffranke adds that recently "important breakthroughs in the field of instrumentation have elevated aura research to a new branch of modern science—a branch of growing importance in Europe."

The first scientific proof of the existence of the aura was attempted by Dr. Walter J. Kilner in 1908. This physician of St. Thomas' Hospital in London was doing some electrical experiments and chanced to use a viewing filter stained with dicyanin dye. Through it he saw hazy outlines around people, and these, he suspected, might be analogous to auras. He began to experiment and developed eventually two screens made of glass cells filled with an alcoholic solution of dicyanin. This arrangement made auras so plainly visible that Dr. Kilner was able to spend years studying them. In 1920 he published a book, *The Human Atmosphere (the Aura)*, in which he stated that he was firmly convinced that the study of the aura physically would gradually come to the fore as one of the aids to diagnosis of human ills. (It looks now as if this prediction is beginning to come true among Europeans, according to Schaffranke.)

Dr. Kilner wrote: "Hardly one person in ten thousand is aware that he or she is enveloped by a haze intimately connected with the body, whether asleep or awake, whether hot or cold, which, although invisible under ordinary circumstances, can be seen when conditions are favorable." He believes that 95 out of 100 people with normal eyesight can learn to see the aura, adding that "One gentleman states that only one person out of 400, to whom he had tried to show the aura, was unable to distinguish the phenomenon."

What Dr. Kilner saw through his glass was a cloud of radiation extending for about six to eight inches around each nude body, showing distinct colors. It varied in size and shape both in health and disease, for such factors as ill health, fatigue, and depression made it alter in distinctness, size, and color. It could be influenced by external forces such as electricity and chemical action.

Since Kilner's time a number of investigations have been made to try to determine if there are unknown radiations emanating from the human body, and the conclusion is that the body is surrounded by electrical or electro-static fields.

Clairvoyants, who do not know an electro-static field from a soccer field, also confirm these findings, seeing radiations in the form of auras encompassing almost anybody. Dr. Gerda Walther, a psychic of Munich, Germany, says, "Usually the aura seems to surround the person to whom it belongs like a kind of incorporeal 'spiritual' cloud, corresponding more or less with the outlines of the individual's physical body, depending on the spiritual and intellectual stage of development of the person involved. Thus, for example, highly developed persons seem to have auras which extend far beyond their bodies."

Dr. Walther has observed auras since 1915, long before she knew what they were. She says, "From the very outset I received a definite impression of a person's character from his aura. Only later did I learn that Oriental philosophies and some of the newer occult doctrines describe auras in the same way as I saw them; and they attribute to them almost the same characteristics as I seemed to see in them."

With reference to the color of auras, Dr. Walther explains that one and the same color may mean something quite different in different auras. "When I say that an aura is blue, I may mean any one of countless shades of blue. It also makes a fundamental difference if the same color is more or less shining and translucent or dull and opaque, like a body-color in painting.

"The actual color involved may be approximately the same, yet there is a world of difference between the 'yellow' of a painted wall and that of a sunbeam. The same thing is true of the colors of an aura."

The fact that various persons describe the aura differently could be because of the possibility that there are several different auras; at least some authorities, particularly occultists, claim so. Or perhaps there is one major aura with different interpenetrating parts or layers. Theosophists list as many as twenty-one different subdivisions.

The ability to see auras and/or surrounds is one of the first recognized skills of a developing psychic, although it actually may be learned by ordinary citizens if they put their minds to it. There is a little trick I have been shown whereby it is possible to see an indistinct emanation, whatever it be termed, coming from the body:

Stand a person dressed in dark clothing before a blank wall in a very dark room which has a minute amount of indirect lighting. Then, if the proper balance of light and dark has been achieved, you will see a tiny radiation surrounding the head and hands. From what I gather, this may be only the manifestation of inward energy; and there may be much more to see, if only we had the curiously endowed eyes of a clairvoyant.

Think of the problems life must present to those who are born able to see auras and surrounds—who from earliest childhood see everyone ringed in a fuzzy fringe of light. It did not become obvious to Eileen Garrett that she was viewing things differently from others until she was in school.

"I was often accused of lying by both teachers and schoolmates," she tells us in *Adventures in the Supernormal*. But, she adds, "I still clung to my own knowledge which existed for me beyond the reach of their perception."

Young Eileen saw people "as if each were set within a nebulous egg-shaped covering of his own. This surround, as I called it for want of a better name, consisted of transparent changing colors, or could become dense and heavy in character—for these coverings changed according to the variation in people's moods. I had always seen such surrounds encircling every plant, animal and person, and therefore paid less attention to the actual body contained within. When I referred to these misty surrounds, no one knew what I meant, although it was very difficult for me to believe that others did not see them enveloping each living organism."

Even after she was grown, this strange power remained with Mrs. Garrett, with occasional additional attributes. She says in *Awareness*, "I was one day surprised and disturbed to perceive a shadowy replica of myself at some distance in front of me. After observing it for a moment, I rose and attempted to approach that alter ego; and as I did so it lost outline and drew back toward me. It was my own 'surround.' I have since learned that it could be expanded."

In her writings Mrs. Garrett never mentions having seen "the cord" and those who have spontaneous projections seldom discuss it; but many regular etheric wayfarers do. Muldoon describes it for us: "The astral and the physical bodies are invariably connected by means of a sort of cord, or cable, along which vital currents pass. Should this cord be severed, death instantly results. The only difference between astral projection and death is that the cord is intact in the former case, and severed in the latter."

This astral umbilical cord is said to be whitish in color and sometimes luminous. It is not rigid, and not fibrous, and is apparently composed of the same material as the etheric body. Descriptions of its size vary with different accounts, and this is probably because the cord is said to be elastic to an almost infinite degree, and the longer it is pulled out, the thinner it becomes.

Muldoon goes on: "The diameter decreases in proportion to the increase of separation of the bodies, up to a given distance, where it is then at its minimum diameter, which it retains from there to infinity—its caliber then being about that of an ordinary sewing thread." On the return trip it increases in size as the astral approaches the physical.

Most writers with experience in this area refer to the cord as a lifeline because it is the contact which means life to the escaping astral form. Muldoon makes just the opposite distinction—he considers the cord necessary because it carries "an intrinsic cosmic energy from the astral, or animate, to the physical, or inanimate."

It is this psychic cord which is credited with enabling Yogis to remain buried for long periods of time. The greatest practitioners of conscious astral projection, Yogis claim vast perfection in the art. When the physical body is interred, they assert that it is the astral cord which supplies a continuous life current to the inert organism in the ground. The conscious mind then, in the astral body attached to the cord, travels and gains knowledge of other places and things—sometimes for days on end.

And so, in this chapter we have been told that penetrating and surrounding the complex of energy called the human physical body, there is a complex of energy of different composition and characteristics but similar shape and appearance (to those whose eyes are endowed with the certain attributes necessary to see it, or to those who have the proper training which makes it apparent). And this, we are assured, is what can leave the body on occasion and have astral projections.

But, you say, this thing which travels outside the body *thinks*, and *is* the actual person, not just a reasonable facsimile of him. The explanation for this is that on most of its jaunts the astral body is accompanied by the *conscious mind*. Yet testimony indicates that even this is variable; and that the consciousness seems able to remain at home under certain unknown conditions. Evidence that the astral body sometimes projects without the mind are the odd manifestations called doppelgänger and vardøger, to be discussed later. Our astral orbiters insist upon one point, and one point only: that the conscious mind works in and through the astral body and the dense physical body, but that it exists apart from both.

And now, having considered the varying statements of numerous ostensible authorities that there is such a thing as an astral body, we have to do something else which might at first seem strange. We have now to try to establish that man actually does possess a separate entity known as a mind —something that has real and individual existence in its own right and is thus capable of leaving the body at will.

5

To

Find the Mind

PERHAPS A DISCUSSION OF THE BRAIN, MEMORY, AND THE UN-
conscious will help us to understand more about the conscious
mind, with particular reference to its location. Bearing in mind
that we have numerous case histories to indicate that the consciousness is able on occasion and under certain circumstances
to leave the body, let us see first *if* this is physically possible,
according to current information.

We must remember, in assessing the medical data available, that even the greatest doctors and surgeons do not claim
to know much about the mind. This fact is pointed out in
the obituary of the accomplished neurophysiologist Sir Charles
Scott Sherrington in the *Journal of the American Medical Association* for July 26, 1952. Although his genius in explaining
the workings of the spine and cerebral cortex was well-known,
Sherrington "disclaimed any credit for advancing knowledge
of mental functions. When discussing the brain as an organ
of the mind, Sir Charles insisted, as recently as 1947, that we
are no farther along today in accounting for mental processes
in physiological terms than was Aristotle two thousand years
ago."

Because the seat of consciousness has for so long been considered to be trapped in the junglelike vastness of the ten-
billion nerve cells of the brain, hidden alike from psychological
explorers and surgeons armed with scalpel and trephine, our

search for it must begin there. The prevailing concept for many years has been that the mind is merely a manufactured product contrived by the spontaneous activity of the brain substance out of informative data supplied by the five senses, chiefly vision. While definitely not advocating this theory, Dr. Russell G. MacRobert, in an article entitled "Science Studies Intuition" in *Tomorrow* Magazine, enlightens us further about it:

"To orthodox psychology, mental processes are an organization of quasi-electrical and chemical activities confined to the physical brain—under one name or another, this is the 'production' theory. The brain produces thought—secretes it—as the liver secretes bile. Impressions from the outer world come to the sense organs and are transmitted along nerve pathways to the brain and there, in some manner, are transformed into perceptions. The brain is a factory in which perceptions are produced. Memories are regarded as a kind of perception. One of the functions of the brain is to store the perceptions and reproduce them on occasion as recollections.

"As for phenomena other than perceptions, such as imagination, reasoning, purposes and meanings, they have no place in this construction of the mind."

If you can't accept this concept of mind as a secretion of the brain, do not be disheartened. Many people don't. I certainly don't. The testimony of my own experience informs me that there is a specific individual which is the real "me," which resides somewhere back of my eyes. Raynor C. Johnson, Master of Queen's College, University of Melbourne, who agrees, discusses such an entity with great clarity in *The Imprisoned Splendour*:

"Consciousness is a fundamental idea which cannot be defined—yet without it nothing else can be defined. It is unlike all else in that it is at once subject and object. It is, and it knows that it is. To talk of perceptions, feelings, thoughts, memories, etc., as the stream of consciousness is wrong: they are a stream of experience. Consciousness, or the 'I,' is conscious only of itself, but it is *aware* of that which constitutes the not-self. Perceptions, feelings, thoughts and memories are parts of 'I's' experience; they are an intimate part of it, for they constitute his empirical self or personality or Ego. His central, unchanging, transcendental self or essence is what we have called 'I' or the true Self."

Now, I know that this "I" or consciousness is, in a way, completely separate from my body, the majority of whose functions are not controlled by me consciously in any way. Still, I know that my mind is able to function only because of and through the apparatus of the body, and that my mental condition depends very much on the health of that body. Whatever it is that thinks "I" in any one of us is not a constant, unchanging reality, as is brought out by Professor Hornell Hart in *The Enigma of Survival*. "Nor is it something which progresses smoothly and consistently along a regular trend," he says. "Rather (at least in the great majority of people) the I-thinker observes clearly at certain times but very foggily at others; it may be seeing only the bright side of everything one day and only the gloomy side the next. Furthermore the actions of this essential self may be aggressive at one time and submissive at another—and may vary in countless other ways.

"Sometimes the moods and attitudes of the essential self may be traced to psychological experiences of success or failure, or the like. But at other times the chemical contents of the blood stream may be directly responsible. The behavior of an intoxicated man, for example, is largely determined by the amount of alcohol in his blood."

And so, Hart goes on, "To look at the body-mind problem without bias, it is essential that we recognize two pivotal facts: 1. that damage to brain structure may block or distort what the I-thinker wants to transmit; and 2. that the chemical condition of the brain has marked effects on the moods and attitudes of the I-thinker himself." Hart, admitting that his analogies are much too crude, says, "Just as a broken connection on a telephone, or a burnt-out fuse in a television set might stop the flow of communication without in any sense impairing the consciousness of the person seeking to transmit, so various sorts of damage and disorder to the brain would obviously be expected to produce interference, no matter whether the brain is a generator or a transmitter of consciousness."

In perusing various works which deal with this subject we find that there are differing points of view. Dr. Gardner Murphy, Director of Research of the Menninger Clinic, suggests in *Three Papers on the Survival Problem* that the specific areas of the brain mediate the specific qualities of experience. "Let the surgeon expose part of the brain in a patient under local anesthesia," he says, "probing electrically here and there; he may elicit in the patient specific experiences of warmth, cold, touch, by stimulating those regions which have long (on anatomical grounds) been assigned to the mediation of these same experiences of warmth, cold, touch. Injury, moreover, to specific regions of the brain may obliterate the capacity to experience the corresponding warmth, cold, touch sensations, just as injuries to the auditory or visual centers may cause disturbance, or even loss, of auditory or visual experience."

For Dr. Murphy it is difficult to think of any conscious process except in terms of the total dynamic adaptive process thus mediated by the nervous system. "The biological point of view makes it difficult to think of *any aspect of awareness* as continuing independently of the very substratum which has given it its place in nature," he says, and concludes: "Mind and body are not things about which we have *ultimate* knowledge, nor can we say that one is the 'cause' of the other. They might perhaps best be conceived as two aspects of one fundamental unity, the ultimate nature of which we are not likely to guess for a long time. But it is extremely difficult, from a biological point of view, to conceive what is meant by referring to personality as *independent* of the living organism—so as to survive beyond death—for the living organism is a psychophysical unity."

Nobel Prize-winning French philosopher and physiologist Henri Bergson couldn't agree less. He maintains that consciousness is *not* a function of the brain. Memory, he says, is of the nature of spirit, and memories are a part of the mind itself. He believes that there are no memory centers in the brain and that pathological changes in the brain simply prevent the memories from actualizing themselves. He comments that there is no real loss of memory from a brain lesion.

Observation of certain patients would tend to back him up. Occasionally we hear of persons in comas who have awakened to a moment or two of consciousness before lapsing into the traumatic condition. I have a friend whose father was for many months before his death in an almost vegetative state, his brain destruction so complete that doctors assured the family that even if he lived he would never be himself again. However, on two different occasions he suddenly awoke and spoke in a perfectly normal manner. Once he said to his wife, who was at his bedside, "I am giving you a great deal of trouble, aren't I, dear?" He then conversed with her about other things before falling back into his previous state.

Dr. Carl Jung, in his work on synchronicity, tells of a woman who was in a deep coma, from which she ultimately recovered. Then she assured him that during her coma she had registered everything taking place in the room as though she were looking down from the ceiling. She saw herself lying in the bed, deathly pale, with closed eyes. Her "detached soul," disengaged from her body, was able to make perceptions in no way inferior to those of actual and wide-awake senses. "These experiences seem to show," Jung said, "that in swoon states, where by all human standards there is every guarantee that conscious activity and sense perceptions are suspended, consciousness, reproducible ideas, acts of judgment, and perceptions can still continue to exist."

This very idea is now beginning to receive support from, of all people, neurosurgeons; and it is suspected by various others who are studying and working with patients who have suffered brain damage of one kind or another.

Neurologists have not yet agreed on a detailed mapping of brain areas, and they do not know what parts of the brain are responsible for controlling various movements, functions and faculties, from aimless thumb-twiddling to an ability to comprehend higher mathematics. They do know that in the normal right-handed person the left hemisphere of the brain is dominant. But, according to *Time*, January 11, 1963:

"While mapping with the help of electronic stimulation has pinpointed some parts of the brain primarily responsible for controlling individual parts of the body as small as the tongue, fingers, or even eyelids, there is evidence of much overlap and feedback. Speech obviously demands control of movements of different parts of the mouth—but not until after the speaker has decided what words he wants to say. So both motor control and intellectual processes would appear to be involved.

"If medical scientists had to rely on the study of healthy people to find out how the brain works, they would know even less about it than they do. But an accident in a brain artery is one of the most dramatic and disabling illnesses that can befall a man. And in the U.S., it is one of the most common. Each year, a million or more Americans suffer strokes and other forms of brain damage, with 200,000 deaths resulting. From the study and treatment of stroke victims, researchers are learning the implications of using half a brain, and what can be done when that half is damaged."

For a cure "Medicine can only rely on whatever self-healing capacity the damaged brain area has—or find some way to stimulate another part of the brain to take over the functions of the damaged part."

The fact that often more or less complete rehabilitation is possible even after a patient's seemingly total paralysis shows that the mind itself was not affected. Other evidence that consciousness cannot be identified with the brain includes the numerous cases of persons who have continued to think normally with large areas of their brains damaged or destroyed. Dr. Gustave Geley in *From the Unconscious to the Conscious* quotes a number of such cases, among which are the following:

"M. Edmond Perrier brought before the French Academy of Science at the session of December 22, 1913, the case observed by Dr. R. Robinson of a man who lived a year, nearly without pain, and without any mental disturbance, with a brain reduced to pulp by a huge purulent abscess."

From the clinic of Dr. Nicholas Ortiz in Bolivia come certain cases whose authenticity, Geley says, cannot be doubted because they proceed from two authorities of high standing in the scientific world.

"The first case refers to a boy of 12 to 14 years of age, who died in full use of his intellectual faculties although the encephalic mass was completely detached from the bulb, in a condition which amounted to real decapitation. What must have been the stupefaction of the operators at the autopsy when, on opening the cranial cavity, they found . . . a large abscess involving nearly the whole cerebellum, part of the brain and the protuberance. Nevertheless the patient, shortly before, was known to have been actively thinking. . . .

"The second case is not less unusual. It is that of a native aged 45 years, suffering from cerebral contusion at the level of Broca's convolution, with fracture of the left temporal and parietal bones. Examination of the patient revealed rise of temperature, aphasia [loss of speech], hemiplegia [paralysis] of the right side. The director and physicians of the clinic undertook an interesting experiment in re-education of speech; they succeeded in getting him to pronounce consciously and intelligibly eight to ten words." Unfortunately the patient died before any further tests could be attempted. The autopsy revealed a large abscess occupying nearly the whole left cerebral hemisphere. "In this case also," Geley says, "we must ask, how did this man manage to think? What organ was used for thought after the destruction of the region which, according to physiologists, is the seat of intelligence?

"A third case, coming from the same clinic, is that of a young agricultural laborer, eighteeen years of age. The post mortem revealed three communicating abscesses, each as large as a tangerine orange, occupying the posterior portion of both cerebral hemispheres, and part of the cerebellum. In spite of these the patient thought as do other men, so much so that one day he asked for leave to settle his private affairs. He died on re-entering the hospital."

The famous American crowbar case, a classic example of tremendous brain destruction without the mind being affected, comes to us via DeWitt Miller's *You Do Take It With You* from *Anomalies and Curiosities of Medicine* by Gould and Pyle. Miller writes:

"Phineas Gage, a young foreman of a railway construction gang, was using a crowbar to charge a hole with powder, preparatory to blasting. Somehow the powder exploded prematurely and the crowbar was driven entirely through Gage's head. The bar was an inch and a quarter in diameter and weighed thirteen pounds."

Gage did not lose consciousness and walked up a flight of stairs seeking medical attention. When the bar was removed and the broken bone cleared away, there remained a hole three and a half inches in diameter in his skull. A gaping opening, caused by the penetration of the bar, transfixed Gage's brain. "Despite the destruction of such a huge amount of brain tissue," Miller reports, "he remained rational throughout his convalescence, which was uneventful. His recovery was complete, except that he lost the sight of one eye. He lived for many years after the accident, his life being normal and his mental faculties unimpaired."

Brain surgeons now, with impunity, perform massive amputations of brain parts which psychologists have considered essential for thought and memory. In 1922 Dr. Walter Dandy of Johns Hopkins Hospital in Baltimore informed his colleagues in the medical profession that he had removed large portions of the brains of living human beings without any apparent defect in intellectual function. This report so intrigued Dr. Wilder Penfield (now professor emeritus of neurology and neurosurgery, McGill University) that he began a long series of analyses himself.

In 1932 Penfield reported the removal of the whole right prefrontal lobe of the brain. He noted that the patient had not only remained conscious throughout the entire operation, but talked normally and rationally to the surgeons concerning her children and other daily matters.

During the years that followed, Dr. Penfield continued his researches. By means of a weak electrical current he temporarily paralyzed various areas of the brain. The whole conception of localization in the brain of mental functions came apart under his electrodes. Dr. Penfield states that he also searched in vain for the seat of memory; and consciousness too refused to identify itself with brain tissue except for two tiny areas. He stated that consciousness is not abolished by paralyzing cells in any part of the brain with the exception of a minute area in the thalamus and a connected small area at the base of the prefrontal lobe.

"Although an individual may be paralyzed, blind or dumb as the result of cortical removal," Dr. Penfield and Dr. Herbert Jasper wrote in 1947, "he nevertheless remains introspective, reflective, aware." Furthermore, "Even the anterior frontal lobe may be completely removed under local anesthesia without seeming to disturb consciousness, and isolation of both lobes by the lobotomy guillotine does not abolish it."

In March, 1950, Dr. Penfield, lecturing at Johns Hopkins University, and now backed by five hundred experimental cases, virtually challenged psychologists to discard disproved theories of mind-brain relationship and find new ones consonant with the newly discovered facts of cerebral physiology. He said, ". . . the startling discoveries should have profound significance in the field of psychology, providing we can interpret the facts properly." "Perhaps," he added, "we will always be forced to visualize a spiritual element . . . a spiritual essence that is capable of controlling the mechanism." Dr. Penfield concludes, "However far our successors in these studies may go, it is my belief that the machine will never fully explain the man, nor mechanisms the nature of the spirit."

Putting this idea in another way, in *Physical Basis of Mind* Dr. Penfield said, "The patient would agree that something else finds its dwelling-place between the sensory complex and the motor mechanism, that there is a switchboard operator as well as a switchboard."

Now, somewhere in this mental morass we also have to consider the subconscious—that aspect of the human mind which psychologists credit with such astounding capacities and dimensions that it can encompass everything which they cannot explain in any other way. Dr. MacRobert says, "While psychiatry accepted the philosophic abstraction of an unconscious mind, no surmise as to its location has been hazarded, because anatomically there was no evidence. This is their problem: where is man's unconscious mind which is also a vast repository of instinctive tendencies, hereditary influences, and personality determinants, to say nothing of the host of buried memories possible of recall? Can it be in the thalamus?

"The small space occupied by the thalamus (less than one three-hundredth part of the brain) could not possibly contain the billions of sensory impressions preserved from birth onward, as well as carry out the functions of reasoning, feeling, and generally preserving personality. There is a strong possibility that the thalamus holds only the gateway for the ingress and egress of consciousness. Thus, William James' theory of the brain as an organ for the transmission of consciousness and mind, rather than its production, once again becomes important."

And so "the conclusion is that mind has not been eradicated by anesthesia, hypnotic trance or sleep, alcohol, drug or fever intoxicants, nor by the deliria associated with the terminal stage of certain illnesses. Drugs and other intoxicants merely prevent the mind from expressing itself through the brain.

"The foundation for the materialistic view of mind has disappeared because no tissue seems to be necessary to preserve memory. Thus, the chief stumbling block to the acceptance of [extrasensory perception] has been removed."

So "now," Dr. MacRobert concludes, "that recent surgical and electrographic experiments on the brain apparently have demonstrated that the mind is more than the sum of the physical parts of the body, the door is opened to broader views."

With this in mind, let us now take an *extremely* broad view for a moment. Now that we have allowed the doctors their say, may we listen to someone else who wants to express himself on the subject albeit by a very long-distance telephone? The fact that this gentleman passed from the earth in 1901 and that his statement was received through the medium Geraldine Cummins in the 1930's may make us somewhat distrust his account, but let's give him the courtesy of listening, anyway. One of the founders of the Society for Psychical Research, the brilliant F. W. H. Myers, at your service:

"Mind does not work directly on the brain. There is an etheric body which is the link between mind and the cells of the brain . . . far more minute corpuscular particles than scientists are yet aware of travel along threads from the etheric body, or double, to certain regions of the body and to the brain . . . I might call them life units. . . . This invisible body —called by me the double or unifying mechanism—is the only channel through which mind and life may communicate with the physical shape. Should a thread snap between the two, there is immediately a failure in control. . . .

"Each animal has a unifying invisible body made out of modified ether. It should be possible to devise in time an instrument whereby this body can be perceived."

If psychologists cannot agree and give us an intelligible explanation of what the mind is and how it works; if surgeons cannot designate where the mind is located, or prove that it is fixed in tissue; can we then affirm that this entity claiming to be Myers, whoever or whatever he is in his current state, may not know what he is talking about?

Even if he is right, and mind is a component of the astral body instead of the physical, it hasn't explained to us what mind is, where memories are stored (the universal subconscious?) or how a mind uses the brain for its purposes. But that is not actually our problem in this book. Our query is whether or not the mind might legitimately leave the body on occasion. If we have no assurance from medical practitioners that the mind is actually locked up in the skull, then we should feel more free to conjecture about its travelling ability, shouldn't we?

If this obscure and elusive entity known as the human mind is ever captured and identified and located in space, it may turn out to be exactly as peripatetic as our astral excursionists maintain it is.

6

Travelling Clairvoyance

DO WE HAVE ANY ACTUAL PROOF THAT THE MIND, WHICH WE have just been attempting to liberate from the brain, does go gadding about? Not exactly. Of evidence, we have plenty; proof, no—because there is always our Devil's Advocate to remind us that some hypothesized form of super ESP could account for the same phenomenon. However, in the examples of travelling clairvoyance, or extrasensory travel, we have some highly interesting material which we should not be too quick to underestimate just because someone can postulate some theory to top it.

Beginning with a small case in which information is obtained during a spontaneous out-of-body experience, we have the story Mr. W. E. Manning of Lisson Grove told me one day in the office of the Society for Psychical Research in London. Mr. Manning said that he was quite familiar with the seaside town of Brighton, having visited there on numerous occasions. One night he travelled there again while lying in his bed in London. He does not remember the exact date, but it was a few years before World War II, and he was awake enough to be critical about whether he was dreaming or having an astral flight. He knew it was the latter, because he's had them before. He told me, "I thought I was in Brighton and saw several windmills. I said to myself that there were no windmills in Brighton."

This confused Mr. Manning mightily. He was sure he was not dreaming, sure he was awake and having an out-of-body experience, sure he was projected to Brighton, and equally sure he was looking at windmills. And there were no windmills in Brighton! What a contretemps. He learned later, he told me, that in connection with an advertising stunt for the Town Council of Brighton some temporary windmill structures had been erected, and they were there at the time of his unconventional visit.

The distinction between ordinary clairvoyance (which is perception of facts, things, or conditions without the use of the normal senses) and the travelling kind is evident here, for in the latter the subject actually believes himself to be present at the scene where the information is gathered. Even when he does not say that he is there, he may make statements which indicate that he thinks he is, or he may have a distinct feeling of coming back into his body afterwards.

Eileen Garrett has attempted to describe in *Tomorrow*, Autumn, 1963, the changing points of view experienced by an astral traveler. Some of her best results were achieved when Dr. Anita M. Mühl and others who have worked with her asked her to visualize their European friends and acquaintances about whom she knew nothing normally.

"Once I was bidden to go out and explore for information," Mrs. Garrett says, "I had a sense of all barriers being removed. The process of projecting oneself away from one's own being and one's own particular surroundings was an exciting release. All barriers of thought were laid aside for the moment, and one travelled into a cosmic flow of light where ideas, smells, associations, even a sense of warmth or cold as one journeyed, gave great pleasure to the senses. It soon became easy to interpret the emotions of people at a distance, to take stock of their surroundings and to bring back an objective story."

The most productive of all Mrs. Garrett's clairvoyant travels is described in her book *My Life as a Search for the*

Meaning of Mediumship, when a test was set up in 1934 between Dr. Mühl in New York and Dr. D. Svenson, the Mental Health Chief in Reykjavik, Iceland. To protect the anonymity of the experimenters, they were not named in the book, and "Newfoundland" was substituted for "Iceland."

Mrs. Garrett, in New York, was supposed to visit Dr. Svenson in Reykjavik, where he had set up certain test conditions. She explains her *modus operandi:*

"While I am in a state of projection, the double is apparently able to use the normal activity of all five senses which work in my physical body. For example, I may be sitting in a drawing room on a snowy day and yet be able in projection to reach a place where summer is at that moment full-blown. In that instant I can register with all my five physical senses the sight of the flowers and the sea, I can smell the scent of the blossoms and the tang of the ocean spray, and I can hear the birds sing and the waves beat against the shore. Strange to say, I never forget the smallest detail of any such experience which has come to me through conscious projection, though in ordinary daily living I can be quite forgetful and memories of places or things may grow dim. . . ."

In her projected state in Iceland she discovered herself able to sense the damp of the atmosphere, and she saw and smelled the flowers growing in the garden by the sea. She passed through the walls and was inside the room in which the experiment was to take place. There was no one there, but the doctor walked down the stairs at that moment and entered.

Dr. Svenson himself had powers of extrasensory perception and was obviously aware of her invisible presence when he walked into the room. Mrs. Garrett writes: "In what I am about to relate, the proof of our mutual awareness will soon become evident. Speaking aloud and addressing me, he said, 'This will be a successful experiment. . . .'"

Then the doctor said, "Now look at the objects on the table." As Mrs. Garrett looked at them with her astral eyes, she described them aloud in New York to the secretary who was sitting beside her taking notes.

She heard Dr. Svenson say, "Make my apologies to the experimenters at your end. I have had an accident and cannot work as well as I had hoped."

And Mrs. Garrett could see that his head was bandaged. She described the bandage. As she did so, she heard with her physical ears a whisper in New York as Dr. Mühl commented in an aside, "This can't possibly be true. I had a letter a few days ago and the doctor was quite well then."

Then Dr. Svenson in Iceland walked slowly to his bookcase. Before he reached it, Mrs. Garrett knew what book he was thinking of and its position on the shelf. He took it down and held it up in his hands with the definite idea that she could read the title, which she did. He then opened it and without speaking read to himself a paragraph out of this volume, which was about Einstein and his theory of relativity. As he silently read the paragraph, she reported the sense of it in her own words to the stenographer in New York.

The experiment took fifteen minutes, and during it evidence was given not only of telepathy, clairvoyance, and precognition, but of the entire range of supernormal sensing. Yet there had also been this additional dimension—Mrs. Garrett's awareness of being on the spot and participating in the reception of evidence: her feeling that she was having an out-of-body experience.

The New York records were posted that night to the doctor in Reykjavik. Next morning a telegram was received from him in which he described an accident which had occurred just before the experiment had begun and which caused his head to be bandaged. A day later a letter from him arrived, listing the steps of the experiment as he had planned it. Every step proved that what she had described was correct.

Not too many people, even those who are able to have astral projections when at home in their quiet little rooms, are able to produce them on command in a laboratory under test conditions. Much less are they able to project to a spot designated by the experimenter and observe the exact material he wishes described. Therefore, most of the most successful tests for travelling clairvoyance have been conducted while the subject was hypnotized. And even then, many of the best cases of this type occurred during the days of mesmerism when more adventurous experimentation was done. (And, the parapsychologist will say, less careful records were kept.)

Travelling clairvoyance produced by hypnosis has not been reported in sufficient detail to make it clear how closely it resembles conventional out-of-body experiences. A few such instances follow, which the reader will note are singularly lacking in description of the actual condition of the subject.

An early and very good case was given in Mrs. Eleanor Sidgwick's paper "On the Evidence for Clairvoyance."

A woman called Jane, the wife of a Durham pitman, so the story goes, was hypnotized at intervals for many years for the sake of her health; and while in trance she would be asked to travel—guided by suggestion to places she should visit clairvoyantly. Once, Dr. F., who hypnotized her, tells us that he had informed one of his patients, a Mr. Eglinton, that he would have Jane call upon him clairvoyantly in his home at Tynemouth, where she, of course, had never been in person. Mr. Eglinton was just recovering from a very severe illness and was thin and weak.

The doctor had described to Jane the place he wanted her to visit. "Before us," he concluded, "we see a house with a laburnum tree in front of it."

She said, "Is it the red house with a brass knocker?"

"No," said the doctor, "it has an iron knocker." (But he later learned that the knocker was brass.)

Jane told the doctor the gentleman she was visiting was named Eglinton, spelling it carefully. Dr. F. had always spelled it "Eglington" and so thought she was wrong in her spelling; but he later learned that it was he, and not she, who was incorrect. She described the gentleman as fat, not thin. She asked if he had a cork leg. She pictured him as sitting by the table with papers beside him and a glass of brandy and water. By then the doctor was completely sure that he was having poor luck with his test, and so he gave up in disgust and brought her out of her trance.

The doctor learned the next day, however, that his friend had found himself unable to sit up so late, and so had ordered a figure to be formed of his clothes. To make the contrast more striking, he'd had an extra pillow pushed under the waistcoat to "form a corporation." The dummy had been placed in a sitting position beside the table, on which were a glass of brandy and water and the newspapers.

One wonders, naturally, why the hypnotized woman could not distinguish between a dummy and a real person; but such are the vagaries of this capricious business. One also wonders why so much of our illustrative material is so whimsical, to wit, the following:

In the *Journal* of the S. P. R., Pierre Emile Cornellier of Paris tells of an experiment conducted in 1915 with a model as his subject. She was hypnotized and asked to find a particular person. She said, "I see him. He is walking barefoot over cold stones." This was a most unlikely statement, but it was afterwards discovered that at that very moment the individual concerned was taking his first treatment of a cure which involved walking barefoot over cold stones.

A much older case was reported by Dr. Walter Franklin Prince in *Noted Witnesses for Psychic Occurrences*, quoting Professor Augustus deMorgan, who has been said by the *Encyclopedia Britannica* to be one of the most eminent mathematicians and logicians of the mid-Nineteenth Century. DeMorgan's wife had on occasion mesmerized a certain little girl in an effort to cure her epileptic fits, and she had discovered that the girl had clairvoyant abilities.

One night the professor dined with friends about a mile from his home—at a house his wife had never visited. When he arrived home Mrs. deMorgan said, "We have been after you." She then told him that she had hypnotized her little patient and sent her to the party as an invisible, uninvited guest. The child described several unusual things about the house and people, which were absolutely correct. DeMorgan had not observed the dining room curtains, and could not tell her whether or not they were "red and white and curiously looped"; it remained for his wife, on a subsequent visit, to ascertain that they were.

The girl also said there was wine and water and biscuits on the table. DeMorgan says, "Now my wife, knowing that we had dined at half-past six, and thinking it impossible that anything but coffee could be on the table, said, 'You must mean coffee.' But the child persisted, 'Wine, water, and biscuits.'" She was right, of course.

DeMorgan was so impressed that he said for publication, "All this is no secret. You may tell whom you like, and give my name. What do you make of it? Will the never-failing doctrine of coincidence explain it?"

His enthusiasm is most heartwarming. But unfortunately, such incidents seem relatively rare nowadays, primarily because hypnotists don't think of taking the time and effort to make the appropriate tests. And so it is that we salute Dr. John Björkhem, even though we can't read his book about his experiments. This Swedish psychiatrist's report on his studies has not yet been translated into English; but I understand that in the past few years he has made over three thousand tests in an attempt to confirm the existence of travelling clairvoyance. As is to be expected, he has found that in *almost* every case he investigated the subject merely hallucinated or produced a fantasy. Nevertheless, a certain few of his people have displayed the ability to travel clairvoyantly and produce verifiable data.

One of his subjects with exceptional ability once described to him a scene in her home several hundred miles away. She told what her parents were doing and even mentioned a special item in the newspaper that her father was reading. Shortly after this test was over her parents telephoned, frightened because her apparition had just appeared to them.

Miss Margaret Eastman, of the Psychophysical Research Unit, Oxford University, in her paper "Out-of-the-Body Experiences" in *Proceedings*, S. P. R., reasons that "the most we are justified in inferring from accounts of this kind is that some sort of extrasensory perception has occurred. We cannot also infer that in order to obtain the extrasensory information the subject had to leave his body. . . ."

Then what about the fact that the girl's parents also saw her, in a reciprocal kind of thing? Even these can be explained solely in terms of ESP, for the person seeing the one having an out-of-body experience could simply have been receiving telepathic information about the contents of the percipient's mind—which happened at that particular moment to involve him. "There *need* be nothing more to it than that," says Miss Eastman; but she doesn't recommend that anyone be deterred one whit from further investigation which might prove that there *is* more to it than that.

One of these undeterred is Jarl Fahler, president of the Society of Psychical Research in Finland, who has reported outstanding success with testing for travelling clairvoyance. On one occasion in 1953 Fahler asked his subject, whom he calls Mrs. S., for information about a certain Mr. X., whom she knew by sight but about whose private affairs she was completely ignorant. He asked if Mr. X. would shortly be going abroad, and she replied that it depended on many things, but that he was waited for in many parts of the world. Questioned further, she described in some detail an Italian man who was staying at a hotel in London while awaiting Mr. X. His name, she said, was printed in the left-hand corner of the paper on which he was writing. It was PIOVENE (a pseudonym). He was using a fountain pen, not writing in script but printing each letter separately. She also spoke of his agitated manner, of seeing him drumming his fingers on the table and fidgeting with a pin. She said that although the man looked like a good fellow Mr. X. should be cautious in his dealings with him.

Fahler confirmed that Mr. X. did know a man named Piovene, whose appearance and habits coincided accurately with the description given by the subject. This man was waiting to see Mr. X., and on the date concerned was staying at the Savoy Hotel in London. Fahler says, "The next time Mr. X. visited Finland he told me that he was sorry he had not taken Mrs. S.'s warning (to be very cautious with Piovene) for he now had very good reasons to regret it."

In cases of psychic excursion Mrs. S. always—when she was successful—believed that she herself was present at the scene of the events described, and experienced a distinct sensation of coming back into her body afterwards. Simeon Edmunds, who tells of some of his hypnotic investigations in "The Higher Phenomena of Hypnotism" in *Tomorrow* magazine, confirms this: "The most successful subjects in experiments I have conducted myself have also reported experiencing these feelings."

Vince Molloy of East Charles Street, Baltimore, Maryland, has attempted hypnotic assays of this kind with what he considers to be great success. In an article in *Fate* magazine, July, 1963, Molloy describes tests conducted with his friend Lee Thompson, an excellent subject.

One night Molloy hypnotized Lee at his home in Baltimore and told him to travel astrally to the house of George Ellis in suburban Catonsville. Molloy himself had never been there and knew nothing about the Ellis home, so he called Ellis on the telephone to check with him the descriptions Lee would give. Lee described the bungalow, then walked inside, giving correct comments as he went. He then said he had entered the dining room, where, "Over in the corner is a short, dark-haired man standing, talking on the telephone. Above his head is the beginning of an arch that continues over to the other wall. It acts as a room divider between this and the living room."

Then he added, "By the way, that man over in the corner just sat down."

Molloy asked Ellis on the telephone if he had heard what Lee had said. George replied, "Yes, Vince, I heard him. And do you know what? I did just sit down!"

It is encouraging, in this day when most experimentation of this nature seems to be done in either Swedish or Finnish, to hear Molloy say in standard English, "Several of my subjects are able to produce this unusual phenomenon while under hypnosis, and so it is my conclusion that this type of ESP would not be so unusual if more people were hypnotized and tested."

We can only hope that Mr. Molloy, before he and his excellent subject lose touch, will get together with a group of parapsychologists who can devise some controlled trials for them to attempt.

7

ESP

Projections

EVEN MORE CONCLUSIVE THAN TRAVELLING CLAIRVOYANCE, WHICH is pretty good in its own right, are certain ESP projections where an individual consciously decides to make himself seen at a distant place and succeeds in doing so. There are a number of excellent instances of this, some documented by witnesses.

For a simple example taken on the word of the percipient, we have no less an authority than the late Sax Rohmer, novelist creator of the sinister Dr. Fu Manchu, that "not only can we send thought messages, but our bodies too."

"I know," Rohmer says, "because I have done it myself. It took me weeks of practice, concentrating at the same time each day, memorizing the exact route between my study and a friend hundreds of miles away. Finally I succeeded, 'projected' myself by means of thought across the sundering miles. My distant friend knew nothing of the experiment. Yet he told me later that at that exact moment he had seen me, plainly, standing beside him." We also have Sax Rohmer's blithe assurance that "given concentration, almost anyone can do this sort of thing."

Another who attempted "this sort of thing," with perhaps less successful results, is reported by Dr. Robert Crookall, who was at one time Principal Geologist of H. M. Geological Survey, London, and who is now one of the busiest collectors of out-of-body experiences. Dr. Crookall writes in the *Journal,*

S.P.R., September, 1963, that he had recommended to Mr. Edward G. West, a Quaker, of S. Devon, that since he had once been astrally travelling, why not again? Mr. West took him up on this suggestion, later writing his account of it in a letter to Crookall.

West had spent some time at 8:50 p.m. two nights previously concentrating on the idea of visiting an invalid whom he knew to be suffering. He says, "I deliberately visualized herself and condition and tried to add to the vision a cured condition. The concentration lasted a few minutes, and I went on thinking other things." As it later turned out, at that moment the invalid had her eyes shut; but she heard West's voice say, "Would you like me to pray for you?" When she opened her eyes he had gone, but she was so sure that he had been there that she called him on the telephone immediately to report it.

Mr. West was not aware of anything strange or unusual occurring at the time. Neither was Mr. Rose—another who was partially successful. Mr. Rose attempted to visit a friend whom he had previously hypnotized and so felt might be particularly susceptible to his endeavors to make himself seen.

The friend wrote to the *Journal*, S.P.R. her account of his effort to visit her. It follows, in part:

"I lay reading, when suddenly a strange creepy sensation came over me, and I felt my eyes drawn towards the left side of the room . . . there distinct against the curtain was a blue luminous mist." She battled her uneasiness over it and finally turned back to her book. "Soon," she says, "the feeling of fear passed away but all desire for sleep had also gone, and for a long time I lay reading—when again quite suddenly came the dread and the feeling of awe. This time I was impelled to cast my eyes downward to the side of my bed, and there, creeping upwards towards me, was the same blue luminous mist. I was too terrified to move, and remember keeping my book straight up before my face as though to ward off a blow, at the same time exerting all my strength of will and determination not to be afraid—when suddenly, as if with a jerk, above the top of my book came the brow and eyes of Mr. Rose. In an instant all fear left me."

Obviously less appalled by an uninvited man than by a mystifying mist, the lady still didn't approve the intrusion, and she didn't hesitate to say so the next time she saw Mr. Rose. When he came to call the following day she immediately asked him what he had been up to the night before. His answer was, "I went to my room early and concentrated all my thoughts in trying to send my astral body here."

"Well, you can just stop," he was told. "You have been successful, and I didn't like it." How sad, that what might have gone down in history as a stupendous achievement of early scientific investigation into the great principle of astral projection should have been discouraged and suppressed merely because it made a lady nervous.

Although the lady's daughter had also felt that something uncanny was in the room the night of the big experiment, Mr. Rose himself had not been in any way conscious of the success of his attempt. Neither was the Reverend G. Vale Owen when he managed to cause a complete manifestation of himself to appear. In his book *Facts and the Future Life* he relates the instance, which involved an invalid named Mrs. Weblock, who was in almost continual pain and had asked that he say prayers for her.

One afternoon as he was relaxing before starting his rounds he thought of Mrs. Weblock with an intense desire to help her suffering. He writes: "I felt that if I could manage to get there in my spirit-body . . . I might perhaps be able to help her . . . without her being conscious of my presence." He fell into a doze for about fifteen minutes, but when he awoke had no recollection of having dreamed or had any unusual adventure during his sleep.

"But," he says, "early the next week I received a letter from Mrs. Weblock which showed me that I had been more successful in my experiment than I had realized." At the time of his nap he had opened the door of her room in Malvern and walked in, her letter revealed. He stood there a few moments smiling at her, and then he faded away. This unusual attention from her pastor was undoubtedly consoling to the invalid.

The best documented descriptions we have of conscious, purposeful astral projection result from the efforts of Mr. S. H. Beard to make himself evident to his fiancée, Miss L. S. Verity and her two sisters. His first experiment was conducted in November, 1881, when he determined to be present in spirit in the front bedroom in which Miss Verity and her eleven-year-old sister slept. No secretive Peeping Tom he, he was resolved also to make his visit known. But since he made up his mind to try this after he went to bed one night, he had no way to warn them in advance. So what happened was that Miss Verity looked up to see him standing by her bedside and was so terrified she screamed. This woke her little sister, who saw him too. So he had two witnesses of his very first attempt.

As to his technique, Mr. Beard explained in *Phantasms of the Living*, "Besides exercising my power of volition very strongly, I put forth an effort which I cannot find words to describe. I was conscious of a mysterious influence of some sort permeating in my body, and had a distinct impression that I was exercising some force with which I had been hitherto unacquainted, but which I can now at certain times set in motion at will."

At psychical investigator Edmund Gurney's request, Beard sent him a post card when he next intended to try an experiment. And, in fact, Beard wrote to him several times of successful attempts. The results were always independently verified by the ladies. On March 22, 1884, he promised by mail to produce an astral excursion that night; and Miss Verity sent a letter a few days later confirming that she had not only seen his apparition while wide-awake but that he had come forward and stroked her hair.

A series of ESP projections in which not only visionary phenomena appeared but an actual conversation was carried on is related by Muriel Hankey in her book *J. Hewat McKenzie*. It all began like this:

"In 1917 I was spending a weekend with Mr. and Mrs. McKenzie. . . . At that time Mr. McKenzie was laid up with a bad attack of phlebitis, and had had his bed brought down to the sitting-room, where he could receive visitors more easily. I arrived in an unhappy mood which I tried to hide, but McKenzie sensed the condition of tenseness, and pressed me as to the cause. I refused to discuss it. He became just a little testy about my reserve and said, 'Well, my girl, good night! If you won't speak, I can't help you, but if you change your mind, come and tell me.' "

She went to her room on the floor above, and after some time fell asleep, still determined to keep silent about what had caused her emotional upset. But in the morning McKenzie knew all about it! He explained to her that she had travelled astrally in the night and told him her problem. He encouraged her to practice this newly-discovered talent, and he attempted it himself. He and she had many reciprocal out-of-body visits after that.

In November, 1921 McKenzie was again laid up with phlebitis, during a time when he and his wife were living at the College of Psychic Science house in London. Mrs. Hankey writes that one night: "I had the experience of going up the stairs at the college. This going up and down is a strange thing. I was not using the treads of the stairs in the normal way, but was, as it were, floating an inch or so above them, without conscious means of propulsion, but with perfect ease, and it seemed quite a natural function. After a slight tap on the closed door, I entered McKenzie's room (without being aware of how I did this), to experience a sense of shock." The heavy smoke-laden atmosphere was there, for McKenzie, when awake, always had a cigar in his mouth. But the figure in the bed, instead of being propped up with pillows, was slumped down flat, with a sheet drawn over his head. Mrs. Hankey says, "I thought, 'Oh, God, he is dead.' After a moment, wishing to look at him, I drew the sheet gently from his face. There, fast asleep, lay William Hope . . . from Crewe. I puzzled over this strange thing, and wondered what had happened."

The next morning she told McKenzie that she had visited him the night before and he had not been sleeping in his bed. "Billy Hope was in your bed. Isn't that silly?"

McKenzie exclaimed, "Good girl! Hope *did* sleep in my bed last night." The explanation was that at about 11 p.m. Hope had called to say he had missed his last train to Crewe and would like to spend the night. As there was no spare bed, McKenzie had moved into his wife's room and given up his own.

On another occasion Mrs. Hankey awoke to see McKenzie bending over her bed. She lived about a mile and a half from the college at that time. "He seemed as solid and real as though actually there in the body, but I was puzzled because he was wearing a huge 'teddy-bear' woollen overcoat, grey in color. This was utterly foreign to him. Normally he either wore no top coat, or wore one of smooth Melton cloth, dark blue in color, with a velvet collar. I had never seen him in any other type or color of coat. On making the customary report in the morning I told him of his strange appearance. He was very pleased, for he had actually purchased just such a coat the previous afternoon, and had worn it during the evening."

Mrs. Hankey says, "Modern researchers will no doubt severely, and perhaps justly, criticize the happy-go-lucky laxity with which these astral excursions were conducted. A member of the S.P.R. Council dismissed them with a vehement gesture, 'Of no value whatsoever!' because they had not been recorded, annotated, signed, witnessed, and placed in the care of a bank, but only a day-to-day diary was kept. No doubt the incidents are of little value to anyone else, but of infinite worth to me, for I learned that these things can and do occur . . . and can be cultivated."

We certainly have to agree with the psychical researcher who says to Mrs. Hankey, "Shocking that better records were not kept and definite data not immediately recorded!" But nonetheless, Mrs. Hankey may be quoted with impunity, because our book is based on the testimony of witnesses. She is a woman of such integrity that she couldn't be lying about such things; and there would be no point in her making them up as a joke. If she doesn't really have these experiences, she so firmly believes she does; if she lives in such a world of illusion that hallucinations consistently appear real to her, wouldn't somebody have *noticed?*

In this field a fully documented account is a real *pièce de résistance,* and such a one is the Wilmot case. An author must hesitate about using it because it has appeared in every anthology of psychic cases since time began. But it always sneaks into a book anyway, because—let's face it, it is the greatest.

Mr. S. R. Wilmot, a manufacturer of Bridgeport, Connecticut, sailed on October 3, 1863, from Liverpool for New York on the steamer *City of Limerick,* accompanied by his sister, Miss Eliza E. Wilmot. There were terrible storms during the first days of the trip, and on the ninth night Mr. Wilmot had his first refreshing sleep since leaving port.

"Toward morning," he is quoted as saying by Mrs. Sidgwick, p. 41, "I dreamed that I saw my wife, whom I had left in the United States, come to the door of my stateroom, clad in her night dress. At the door she seemed to discover that I was not the only occupant of the room, wavered a little, then advanced to my side, stooped down and kissed me, and after gently caressing me for a few moments, quietly withdrew.

"Upon waking I was surprised to see my fellow-passenger, whose berth was above mine but not directly over it—owing to the fact that our room was at the stern of the vessel—leaning upon his elbow, and looking fixedly at me. 'You're a pretty fellow,' said he at length, 'to have a lady come and visit you in this way.' I pressed him for an explanation, which he at first declined to give, but at length related what he had seen while wide awake, lying in his berth. It exactly corresponded with my dream."

This gentleman was William J. Tait, a sedate 50-year-old man who was most impressed by what he had seen. He told Miss Wilmot about it the next morning. In fact, he asked her if it was she who had come into the room. She was naturally quite taken aback at the query—two gentlemen in the stateroom and she a Victorian maiden.

Mr. Wilmot continues: "The day after landing I went by rail to Watertown, Connecticut, where my children and my wife had been for some time, visiting her parents. Almost her first question when we were alone together was, 'Did you receive a visit from me a week ago, Tuesday?' "

"A visit from you?" said Mr. Wilmot, playing it cool. "We were more than a thousand miles at sea."

"I know it," she replied, "but it seemed to me that I visited you."

His wife then told him that on account of the severity of the weather she had been extremely anxious about him. On the night in question she had lain awake for a long time thinking of him, and about four o'clock in the morning it seemed to her that she went out to seek him. Crossing the wide and stormy sea, she came at length to a low, black steamship, whose side she went up. Then, descending into the cabin, she passed through it to the stern until she found him.

"Tell me," she said, "do they ever have staterooms like the one I saw, where the upper berth extends farther back than the under one? A man was in the upper berth, looking right at me, and for a moment I was afraid to go in; but soon I went up to the side of your berth, bent down and kissed you, and embraced you, and then went away."

The description given by Mrs. Wilmot of the steamship was correct in all particulars, though she had never actually seen it. And her extrasensory visit to her husband was real enough to her to have lifted her spirits for days afterward.

Some readers might still say of such a case, "So what? Of what value is it to prove that a person can leave her body and be seen somewhere else?" I'll let Frederic W. H. Myers give you the answer, as he wrote it (during his lifetime and not through a medium) in his great classic *Human Personality and Its Survival of Bodily Death:*

"In these self-projections we have before us, I do not say the most useful, but the most extraordinary achievement of the human will. What can lie further outside any known capacity than the power to cause a semblance of oneself to appear at a distance? What can be a more central action— more manifestly the outcome of whatsoever is deepest and most unitary in man's whole being? . . . Other achievements have their manifest limit; where is the limit here? The spirit has shown itself in part dissociated from the organism; to what point may its dissociation go? It has shown some independence, some intelligence, some permanence. To what degree of intelligence, independence, permanence may it conceivably attain? Of all vital phenomena, I say, this is the most significant; this self-projection is the one definite act which it seems as though a man might perform equally well before and after bodily death."

8

The Human
Double

SUCH WORDS AS DOPPELGAENGER, VARDOEGER, AND AUTOSCOPY ARE tossed about lightly, if at all. But they should be treated with respect as the names of a rare form of phenomenon—the human double.

Being so subjective, the sighting of the human double is, like visions and illumination, liable to the charge that it is merely hallucinatory. Now all we have to do is is to explain how so many people have such similar hallucinations. A hallucination is a mental image that has the vividness of a sensation, but is not caused by stimulation of the sense organs. Dreams come under this classification—they are oneiric hallucinations; but they are considered to be completely normal because everyone has them. Not a great many people confess to seeing their own doubles. It must be quite a startling sensation. But calling it a hallucination doesn't *explain* it.

Even though we can't account for the existence of the human double, let us take it at its face value and see what it amounts to. First we will consider the vardøger, or forerunner. It is so well-known in Norway as to have an integral place in the folklore of the country; and it apparently is perceived just about as frequently today as it has been in the past. Almost any hour someone somewhere in Norway may hear sounds of the arrival of an invisible person, who is soon to appear in the flesh. The man of the house may be heard to walk up the front steps, open the door, take off his overshoes, put his umbrella into the hall stand, put his hat on the closet shelf, all in the manner in which he is accustomed to act—except that he hasn't really arrived home from work yet. This occurs so often that we are told it is almost taken for granted. In fact, many a housewife begins preparing the dinner after hearing the sounds of her husband's arrival, so as to have everything ready by the time he actually comes home. She knows she can rely on the fact that he is on his way.

Apparently on occasion not only the sound but the actual apparition of an individual may be a forerunner. An importer from New York named Erkson Gorique was in his fifties in 1955 when the account of his first trip to Norway was published in the *New York Herald Tribune*. A successful, widely-traveled businessman, Gorique had decided he would investigate the situation with regard to importing Norwegian china and glassware. He had no relatives in Norway, and, as noted above, had never been there before.

Gorique flew to Oslo in July and registered at the best hotel in the city. As he signed his name the room clerk said, "I'm glad to see you again, Mr. Gorique. It's good to have you back."

"I'm sorry, but I've never been here before," said the importer. "You must have mistaken me for someone else."

The clerk insisted that Mr. Gorique had been in the hotel a few months before to make the reservation for July, and that his unusual name and his appearance had stuck in his mind.

A wholesaler named Olsen was the first businessman Gorique planned to see in Oslo, and when he walked in Mr. Olsen greeted him with, "Delighted to see you again, Mr. Gorique." Olsen said that Gorique's last visit a few months back had been much too short.

The importer was quite upset. Had someone been impersonating him, he wondered? It seemed highly unlikely, for his plans for the trip were known to very few people. Mr. Olsen had an answer for his puzzlement. "Have you never heard of the vardøger, or forerunner?" he asked. He described this phenomenon, with which all proper Norwegians are familiar; but, of course, he could not explain it—no one knows how to explain it for sure.

That the vardøger exists in other countries besides Norway is indicated by an account given by Charles L. Tweedale, who was Vicar of Weston, England, in 1911. He says in his book *Man's Survival After Death*:

"This extraordinary faculty of the projection or excursion of the ego has been manifest in my own person on many occasions during the last few years. Very many times I have been heard to come into the house, open the door of my study, or pass upstairs, my footsteps being plainly audible [to my wife, children, and the servants]. On going to speak to me on these occasions they found no one there, but I invariably arrived a few minutes afterwards. At first I could scarcely believe these accounts, although the witnesses firmly protested their truth. On several occasions I have been seen where my corporeal body was certainly not present at the time. These experiences happened many times, as recorded in my journal, and almost invariably took place when I was hastening home or proceeding to some spot with some fixed purpose in mind."

The instance which Tweedale thinks is the most remarkable and perfectly evidenced occurred on Saturday, October 21, 1911. He had been visiting a parishioner, and had left about 7:30 p.m. and hurried home. On arriving he found the servant and his little daughters, who unbolted the front door to admit him. They excitedly asked him how he had gotten into the house a short time previously, as the door was locked, and how he had gone away again leaving the door bolted on the inside.

"I looked at them in astonishment, asking what they meant, and saying that I had not been in the house for a couple of hours or more," he writes. They said that twenty minutes before he arrived they were all in the kitchen together. Ida, the maid, turned around, saw him come down the passage and stand in the doorway leading to the kitchen, regarding them all intently. He had on his tall hat and long Inverness cloak, and she saw the glint of the light upon his spectacles. She said, "Here's Pa," and all his daughters looked up and saw him. They then observed him turn around and walk up the passage. At that moment the servant remembered that she had bolted the front door. Wondering how he had gotten into the house, they all followed him, but could find no trace of him in the house. They discovered, when they looked, that the front door was still bolted and locked, as also were the back door and all of the windows.

At the time they saw him, Tweedale was actually more than a mile away, hurrying along Weston Lane in the dark, not thinking of home particularly, but feeling ill and tired, trudging doggedly along desiring to get there as quickly as possible. He was wearing his tall hat and Inverness cloak, and had on his spectacles.

"This experience is perfectly remembered by my daughters Marjorie, Sylvia, and Dorothy, who have each written and signed an independent account of it," Tweedale states, appending the signed statements.

His wife had a similar occurrence but in reverse when on May 27, 1922, hastening to speak to him in a room she had just seen him enter, she heard his footsteps *behind* her. Turning around, she beheld him coming out of the room she had just left. "When she was opening the door the other me was close behind her," Tweedale says, "but on looking in she saw me standing at the bookcase and I spoke to her. On turning around she found that the other figure had vanished. This instance is notable in that the footsteps of my double were clearly audible."

Here is another case which is not usually classified as a vardøger, but I don't know why not. An apparition which is also a forerunner is a vardøger, as far as I am concerned. The instance is especially intriguing because it is collective at both ends; and also because we have the word of another preacher as to its authenticity. Poltergeists seem attracted to the clergy; could it be that vardøger are too? It was described by the Reverend W. Mountford of Boston, Massachusetts, and published in *Phantasms of the Living*.

One day Mountford, visiting some friends in Norfolk, stood at a window looking up the road. "Here are your brother and his wife coming," he said. His host and hostess both glanced out, and someone said, "Yes, and look, he has old Dobbin out again," referring to a horse which was just recovering from an accident. Mr. and Mrs. Robert Coe, the people in the buggy, whom they all could plainly see, passed by the house, turned the corner, and disappeared. Everyone was shocked that they should not have stopped in.

A few moments later a young lady entered, pale and excited. "Oh, aunt!" she exclaimed, "I have had such a fright! Father and mother have passed me on the road without speaking!" Her parents had looked straight ahead and never stopped, nor even nodded to her. When she had left home not fifteen minutes before, they were sitting by the fire. She didn't understand what was going on.

While everyone was still discussing this puzzle, the Reverend Mr. Mountford looked out the window once again, as was his wont, and saw the same scene re-enacted; but this time the Coes stopped and came in. They were completely unaware of the turmoil they had caused, for they had left home only ten minutes before and had come directly there.

Mountford does not hazard a guess as to what produced this singular occurrence. Tweedale thinks his were caused by a projection or excursion of the ego. I, myself, am more inclined to favor something in the way of thought forms, of which more later. There are other suggested approaches to the vardøger, among which Professor Wereide's are of interest.

Thorstein Wereide, Professor of Physics at the University of Oslo, is sympathetic toward psychic phenomena because his wife Sophie has been from childhood an extremely highly developed sensitive. He tells us in "Norway's Human Doubles" in *Tomorrow*, Winter, 1955, of several vardøger experiences which involved his wife.

But, once, he himself was the vardøger. He says, "On December 29, 1927, I left home at quarter to three, intending to meet my wife at her office so that we could go together to a shop before going home. As I walked, I began to think I had calculated the time too closely, and that my wife would probably have left the office before I could arrive, so that we would miss each other. Accordingly, I decided to go directly to the shop without meeting my wife, and then go home.

"When I reached home I expected to find my wife there already, but she had not arrived. As a matter of fact, she reached home about an hour later than usual. And the first thing she said when she did arrive was, 'Why didn't you come to my office today? At a quarter of three I saw you come into my room, and I was so certain of what this meant that I decided to wait an hour for you.'"

What it meant was that Professor Wereide had fooled his vardøger by not going to the office where his thoughts had heralded him.

Although psychic phenomena claim no fatherland, Professor Wereide wonders why it is that variations occur which seem to be peculiar to certain specific countries. Not having been apprised of our Reverends Tweedale and Mountford, he believes that the vardøger phenomenon occurs in Norway and Scotland exclusively. He wonders if the special function it has assumed in Norway perhaps has grown out of particular qualities in the Scandinavian personality, or if, quite possibly, it has arisen out of the circumstance of Norway's sparse population. He draws the conclusion that the essential reason the phenomenon appears more often in Norway than in other countries is not because of more frequent projections, but because in Norway a highly developed faculty for sensing and observing the projections is more commonly found.

"Possibly," he says, "the Norwegian people are more disposed toward this particular projection than other people in

Europe, but I believe the dominant factor is that sensitive observers are more nùmerous in Norway."

To follow as many avenues as possible to help us understand such curiosities, I'll quote also a discussion which appeared in *Apparitions and Precognition* by Aniela Jaffé. This disciple of Carl Jung amplifies Wereide's concept by saying, "It is well known that long periods of solitude increase man's ability to turn his gaze within. . . . [In isolation] contents of the unconscious are more easily perceived than in the hurry and bustle of town life." And so the vardøger should be considered as pre-audition or pre-knowledge of an impending arrival. "What really happens is a *duplication of the instant in time*—the future moment takes place now, and once again, at its own time. In other words, it is relativity of time and space in the unconscious which brings about and explains the vardøger phenomenon."

This *explains* the vardøger phenomenon? Well, perhaps not altogether, not even to Miss Jaffé. She goes on to add, "Nevertheless the question remains as to why it is just the arrival of a person that is announced in this way. In isolated districts the arrival retains its original significance of an actual 'encounter,' be it stranger or friend who enters the house. Gestures of greeting as well as the laws of hospitality stress the importance of the incident. *Again it is an archetypal situation which, as we know, may be accompanied by 'supernatural' phenomena.*"

Oh.

Well, whether or not we now understand the vardøger, let us go on to the doppelgänger—a ghost or wraith of a living person. It only seems to vary from the apparitional form of the vardøger in one respect, but that is an important one. The individual involved sees it himself.

Germany's greatest writer, Johann Wolfgang von Goethe, once saw himself as an apparition, and we have his own account of it. It occurred when he was leaving his friend Frederika at Strasburg and riding away on horseback. He writes,

"When I held out my hand to her from my horse the tears were in her eyes, and I felt sad at heart. As I rode away along the foot-path at Drusenheim a strange phantasy took hold of me. I saw in my mind's eye my own figure riding towards me attired in a dress I had never worn—pike grey with gold lace. I shook off the phantasy; but eight years afterwards I found myself on the very road going to visit Frederika, and that, too, in the very dress I had seen myself in, in this phantasm, although my wearing it was quite accidental."

There are several varieties of occurrences which come under the general heading "doppelgänger," or seeing one's own double. In the type just mentioned, the conscious self, remaining in its own body, may see its own phantasm at a distance. This is a phenomenon cited in works on mental pathology, and considered reducible to a pure and simple case of hallucination. Yet, unless Goethe was indulging in poetic license, or pulling our leg, how do we account for the fact that eight years later he discovered himself in that identical position and wearing what he claims to be the very same clothing?

Eileen Garrett, who does not indulge in either poetic license or leg pulling, gives us her word that she had an actual *physical* manifestation as the result of one of her "hallucinations" of this type. One night when she was in Grenoble, France, Mrs. Garrett dreamed that she rose from her bed and went in search of some medication which was on the table in her dressing room. Then she awoke from the dream and watched herself get out of bed, go to the dressing room and search very quietly among the toilet articles on the table. She didn't seem to find what she was looking for. "I only know," Mrs. Garrett says, "that I sat up in bed and watched myself. The experience confused me." She slept then, and when she awoke in the morning the medicine was on the bedside table within reach of her hand. "Which journey to the dressing table found the medication?" she asks. "To this day I have not been able to solve this one."

Illustrating another variation of the doppelgänger is the story told to Professor C. J. Ducasse by Mary Ellen Frallic. Ducasse says in *The Belief in a Life After Death*, "Her 'projection' experience occurred not during sleep or under anesthesia, but while walking on the street. She gradually became conscious of rising higher and higher, up to the height of the second floor of the surrounding buildings, and then felt an urge to look back; whereupon she saw her body walking about one block behind. That body was apparently able to see 'her' for she noticed the look of bewilderment on its face."

So far this is just a simple instance of an out-of-body experience. But there is more. In Miss Frallic's own words, as she wrote them to Sylvan Muldoon for publication in *The Phenomena of Astral Projection:* "A moment later my consciousness suddenly shifted to my physical body, and, looking through its eyes . . . I saw my astral body in space—an exact duplicate of the physical body standing in the middle of the road. This occurred several times." Miss Frallic suddenly, while airborne, realized that she was separated from her physical body and fear gripped her. She stretched out her arms and leaned forward and was quickly drawn towards home base, to which she returned immediately, without repercussion of any kind.

"This all happened within a brief time," she says, "but it *did* happen. . . . By going through this unique, and what was to me an extraordinary experience I understood myself better. . . . It proved to me that man is not alone a material being, but a mental principle."

J. Hewat McKenzie, whom we have already met, had, according to Muriel Hankey, not only a passion for strong cigars but also very strong opinions on everything else. Some of his most enthusiastically held views were on the effects of alcohol and other drugs, particularly anesthetics, on the etheric body as well as on the physical body. To test one of his theories, McKenzie once drank an excess of alcohol in order to discover any of its effects beyond those customarily experienced and condemned. Here is what happened, according to Mrs. Hankey:

"While still able to stand, and consciously to take note, he went into the street and walked along the pavement of a quiet road. He glanced across the street and saw himself walking on the opposite pavement. Thinking he was out of his body, he deliberately crossed the road to rejoin himself, and proceeded on his way. As he turned to look at the pavement on which he had been walking, he saw himself *there*, still walking. He was in a panic of indecision, not knowing which was his physical and which his astral body, as both seemed equally solid to his senses. He was indeed 'a man beside himself.' Fortunately he arrived home in one packet, somehow."

Another of these complicated "back and forth" things occurred to Rosalind Heywood, British psychical investigator and author of two outstanding books on the subject. In *ESP: A Personal Memoir* Mrs. Heywood relates that one night in August, 1921, she was lying in bed thinking about doing something extremely agreeable but entirely selfish. She says:

"Before I could carry out this egoistic idea I did something very odd—I split in two. One me in its pink nightie continued to toss self-centeredly against the embroidered pillows, but another, clad in a long, very white, hooded garment, was now standing, calm, immobile and impersonally outward-looking, at the foot of the bed. This White Me seemed just as actual as Pink Me and I was equally conscious in both places at the same time. I vividly remember myself as White Me looking down and observing the carved end of the bed in front of me and also thinking what a silly fool Pink Me looked, tossing in that petulant way against the pillows. 'You're behaving disgracefully,' said White Me to Pink Me with cold contempt. . . ."

Pink Me furiously retorted, "I shall do what I like, and you can't stop me, you pious white prig!" She was particularly angry because she knew very well that her white counterpart was the stronger and could stop her. "A moment or two later —I felt no transition—White Me was once more imprisoned with Pink Me in one body, and there they have dwelt as oil and water ever since," Mrs. Heywood states.

If one has enough presence of mind, it seems, it is possible to perform experiments with a double. Early in January, 1890, Mr. C. E. G. Simons, then a young medical student, was in Aberdeen, Scotland, studying for an examination. One afternoon, accompanied by two friends, he was in his room, half-lying on the sofa, reading notes on surgery.

Suddenly Simons began to feel, as one sometimes does in a nightmare, as if bound hand and foot. Soon he seemed to himself to be divided into two distinct beings. One of these remained motionless on the sofa and the other moved about. There was what felt like an elastic tension holding the two bodies together. He could make his second body lie on the floor or move to some distance about the room; but at a limit of about two yards he could effect no further separation. During this time he remained fully conscious of all that was going on in the room; he saw his friends moving about and heard someone playing the piano.

The dual condition lasted for about five minutes more, then fusion began to set in. At first Simons resisted this, and found that he could do so with some success. Then he let it continue, and the two bodies united rapidly. He tried to repeat the experience but had no luck. Shortly afterwards he got up and related his story to his two friends. They were amused, and thought that he was just making it up.

The following case, while old, has the advantage of having several witnesses, and this I recommend. If you are ever going to see your own double, make a special point to have as many others there as possible. Mrs. S. J. Hall of Gretton, England, wrote to Edmund Gurney, who at that time was making a collection of "Phantasms of the Living," about an incident which happened to her in the autumn of 1863. Mr. and Mrs. Hall and two visitors were sitting at the dinner table one night when all four of them saw Mrs. Hall standing at the end of the sideboard, dressed in a spotted light muslin dress. It was her husband who first noticed Mrs. Hall's apparition and he exclaimed, "It's Susan." Mrs. Hall says that it seemed as remote from herself and her feelings as a picture or a statue. The dress was not like any that she owned at the time, but she wore one like it some two years later.

(One cannot help but wonder how much having seen himself or herself in a certain costume influences one's unconscious selection at a later date.)

The best thing about a collective case like this is that it lends credibility to others in which one person sees his own double and then for the rest of his life almost goes out of his mind trying to convince his friends that it really happened.

G. N. M. Tyrrell makes a point in his book entitled *Apparitions* which I gratefully appropriate here. It does not explain doppelgängers, but it knocks holes in a lot of the typical arguments that a story like this can arouse. "It has often been pointed out by the collectors of these cases (and the loophole is eagerly seized by those who wish to explain the evidence away), that when one member of a party sees an apparition and makes some remark or exclamation about it, this acts as a suggestion, which causes the others to see the apparition too. But a little reflection will show that this process cannot be at all general; that, in fact, if it ever occurs at all, it must be very rare. Otherwise it would only be necessary to say, 'Look there!' or 'There is so-and-so!' for the person addressed to see an apparition. If this sort of thing really happened the world would become peopled with apparitions to such an extent that one would never be sure who were the living people. . . . As it is, we have evidence that universal suggestibility of this kind does not exist."

Autoscopy is the technical name for the doppelgänger. The double, like the body of the subject of an out-of-body experience, need not duplicate the ordinary body, but, as Margaret Eastman points out, may seem older or younger, solid or transparent. "The physiological circumstances in which autoscopy and out-of-the-body experiences occur are sometimes similar—fatigue, fever, labyrinthine disturbances, epilepsy and migraine," she adds. It may also occur in certain cases of brain damage.

Because of all this, and neglecting to take into consideration the more normal instances such as have been mentioned here, autoscopy is usually regarded by physiologists, psychologists, and many parapsychologists, as a special kind of hallucinatory activity. Although we have quoted some highly reputable people about incidents which seemed to be much more than hallucination, there is always the other side of the coin—those persons who have such oft-repeated or wholesale experiences as to give the whole concept a bad name.

Guy de Maupassant, for example, who eventually died of dementia paralytica, asked his friend Bourget, "How would you feel if you had to go through what I experience? Every other time when I return home I see my double. I open the door and see myself sitting in the armchair. I know it is a hallucination the moment I see it. But isn't it remarkable? If you hadn't a cool head, wouldn't you be afraid?"

The question here is whether de Maupassant's insanity caused him to hallucinate the double; or whether seeing himself as a doppelgänger so constantly is what drove him insane.

9

Bilocation

THE TERM BILOCATION IS TAKEN BY SOME, INCLUDING THE LATE enthusiastic Italian psychical researcher Ernesto Bozzano, to include all the various kinds of out-of-body experiences. Professor Ducasse has a more restricted definition, using the term only in reference to the temporarily excarnate observer who finds himself able to travel away from the vicinity of his body and who may visit a distant place and be reported *to have been seen* at that place at the time.

Limiting ourselves to the use of the word that Ducasse prefers, we will begin our bilocation dissertation with two old cases which are quite well-known, but frankly, I don't know if anyone can say whether or not they are apocryphal.

In Arezzo in 1774 Alfonso de Liguori was in his cell, fasting. On awakening one morning he stated that he had been at the bedside of Pope Clement XIV and that the Pope was dying. Since Clement was in Rome, four days' journey away, Alfonso's story was taken with a grain of the purest Italian salt, until word arrived that the Pope had indeed died.

St. Anthony of Padua was taking his part in the office in one church and was observed to kneel down in his stall and pull his cowl over his head. He remained there some time apparently immersed in prayer, but actually, he had suddenly remembered that he ought to be in another church, so he projected himself there astrally. It was later stated that during the time he appeared to be passive he had been observed to enter the other church and take his part in the office there.

Stories about saints, and candidates for sainthood, gather so much in the telling that they often can seem more fiction than fact. But there are those who will swear that the tales about the contemporary stigmatist Padre Pio are authentic. A Capuchin monk, Padre Pio of Pietrelcina is a legend in his own time, and seems eventually scheduled for sainthood, if his followers have their way. This selfless, humble, and hardworking monk has had the stigmata since 1915, and claims are made that he has performed various miracles of healing.

Padre Pio's biographer, Alberto del Fante, in *Who is Padre Pio?* says that he has also the power to be in several places at once. "What has always seemed to me the most impressive of all the astonishing facts about Padre Pio," he writes, "is the story of Monsignor Fernando Damiani, the Vicar General of Salto, Uruguay. . . . Padre Pio had at one time cured the prelate of a cancer of the stomach, which had made them great friends over the years." Some time later Msgr. Damiani was in Italy, and, as he was now advanced in age, expressed the wish to remain there so that he could die near Padre Pio. But the Padre told him he was destined to return to Uruguay. "I will visit you at the time of your death," he promised.

In 1942 the Archbishop of Montevideo is said to have been awakened by a Capuchin friar who told him to go to Monsignor Damiani because he was dying. Beside the bed was found a note the monsignor had been able to scribble, with the words on it: "Padre Pio came." It is claimed that in 1949 when the Archbishop of Montevideo met Padre Pio in Italy he recognized the Capuchin who had awakened him.

Of Padre Pio's gift of bilocation, Douglas Hunt says in *Exploring the Occult*: "There are many instances similar to his 'visit' to Uruguay. During the First World War General Cardona, who had suffered a defeat, was in his tent meditating suicide when a young monk entered his tent and said, 'Come, General, you would not do anything so stupid.' " At the end of the war the General heard people talking of Padre Pio and went in mufti to his church, San Giovanni Rotondo in Foggia, Italy. When the father passed him, Cardona identified the young monk who had saved him from suicide. Evidently Padre Pio recognized him, too, for he said, "You had a lucky escape, my friend."

Perhaps I should stop while I'm ahead, but Padre Pio stories abound. Unfortunately, another instance too similar to the first can make them both sound dubious. But I'll give it for what it is worth, from the pen of Alberto del Fante. A young lieutenant, attached to a fighter squadron in the last war, one day started off on a mission, but had to bail out when his plane caught fire. The parachute failed to open, and he would have been killed had not a friar caught him in his arms and carried him to earth.

"That evening," Del Fante says, "he told his story to his commanding officer who did not believe a word of it, but gave him a short leave in order to recover from the shock of the experience.

"When he reached home he told his tale to his mother. 'Why, it was Padre Pio,' she said. 'I prayed to him so hard for you!' and she showed him a picture of the Padre. Her son exclaimed: 'Mother! That is the same man!'

"The young soldier went to San Giovanni Rotondo to express his gratitude. Padre Pio said to him: 'That was not the only time I saved you. At Monastir when your plane had been hit, I made it glide safely to earth.'"

Apparently, according to Del Fante, his plane had been hit at Monastir and then managed to float down to safety, but there seemed no way for Padre Pio to have known this normally.

Another Catholic who combines fervent religion with a talent for astral flying is a lay person named Polly, who personally told me several of her experiences. Once, on February 15, 1963, to be exact, her grown son became very ill while vacationing in Sarasota, Florida. His condition was diagnosed as either erysipelas of the brain or spinal meningitis, and it was so critical that after five days his wife finally telephoned their daughter Susan in New York that her father was dying. Susan called Polly, her grandmother, and they decided to pray all day for his recovery.

That night Polly found herself outside her body and floating South, apparently clutching in her hand a bottle containing St. Ann's oil, which had been blessed. It was a bitter cold night, but she was not aware of it as she soared straight for the Memorial Hospital in Sarasota. Quite soon she found herself standing in the doorway of her son's room, and she went up to his bed, caressed him and kissed his feverish face. He opened his eyes and said, "Mom."

Polly answered, "Yes, son, I've come to help you." Then she dipped her thumb into the holy oil and anointed him and made the sign of the cross. He opened his eyes again and smiled. She told him, "You'll be all right now. The doctors will be amazed when they come in. You'll leave the hospital either Tuesday or Wednesday."

Polly came back to consciousness in her own bed, and told her husband her conviction that their son would soon be well. And it was true. He awoke the next morning with no headache and no fever, and he did leave the hospital on Tuesday. When he returned to New York some time later he told Polly, "Mom, I have never been so near death, but something pulled me back. I woke up feeling wonderful the morning after I dreamed that you were there—or were you really there?"

As this story would indicate, it is possible to desire bilocation strongly and achieve it, if you have that special talent required. There seems to be no hard and fast rule to distinguish this from experimental ESP projection. The following instance, taken from the *Journal* of the S. P. R., is experimental as well as reciprocal.

Mr. B. F. Sinclair states:

On the 5th day of July, 1887, I left my home in Lakewood to go to New York to spend a few days. My wife was not feeling well when I left, and . . . I looked back and saw her standing in the door looking disconsolate and sad at my leaving. The picture haunted me all day, and at night, before I went to bed, I thought

I would try to find out her condition if possible. I had undressed, and was sitting on the edge of the bed, when I covered my face with my hands and willed myself at home in Lakewood to see if I could see her [and make her see me]. After a little, I seemed to be standing in her room before the bed, and I saw her lying there looking much better. I felt satisfied . . . and so spent the week more comfortably regarding her condition.

He wouldn't have been so complacent if he had known the anxiety he had caused his wife. For she had seen him the same night in front of her bed, and so had been frantic all week for fear that he had died.

Another reciprocal case, not in the least experimental, just seems to have happened out of the blue, and was entirely unconscious on the part of both projectors. In June, 1905, Mrs. Ellen Green of Manchester, England, was visiting in Llanishen, near Cardiff, Wales, at the house of Frederick Ward, a retired sea captain. Before she left for home on the train, Captain Ward drove her in his trap to Whitchurch, about two miles away, where she spent two days with John Berwick and his wife. Ward returned to Llanishen.

Mrs. Green writes: "On the following afternoon about half-past three I was sitting alone in the drawing room . . . and on happening to look up, I saw Mr. Ward standing at the bay window and looking in at me as though he desired to speak to me. He was in his usual dress and is not a man to be easily mistaken for anyone else. Thinking he had brought some letters for me, I rose hastily and went toward the window calling and waving my hand to him, partly in greeting and partly as a sign for him to go to the hall door; but when I reached the window I was surprised not to see him." He was not at the door either, nor was he anywhere about the house— until the next morning when he arrived to take her to the station, as he had promised. And he was a mess, suffering from injuries to his ankle, neck and shoulders, because a nervous horse had upset the trap two days previously.

Now the thing that makes this story particularly interesting was that on the day before, at the same time that Mrs.

Green had seen Captain Ward's apparition, he had heard *her* voice. He had been lying down resting and in considerable pain, and had heard her outside the front door calling him. He had managed with difficulty to get to the door to admit her, and was greatly surprised when he did not find her waiting on the outside.

While the details of this experience were fresh in their memories, within a few weeks of its occurrence, testimonies were written down for the Society for Psychical Research by Mrs. Green, Ward, and the Berwicks, who had heard both sides of the story, and had heard Mrs. Green's account immediately after she saw Ward's apparition.

Now the last instance of bilocation I will give would indicate that it is possible for a dedicated soul to have such experiences by design and at great frequency. But it is a very old story.

Maria Coronel de Agreda, born in the year 1602, began to have ecstasies when she was eighteen. She was so pious that when she was twenty-five she was made an abbess by a special dispensation from Rome. Her biographers have recounted some of her unusual mystical events at length and Fr. Herbert Thurston quotes them in his book *Surprising Mystics*.

Sister Maria's instances of bilocation—actually as many as 500, according to written accounts—occurred day and night for many months. During these times she believed herself to be transported to Mexico, where she performed missionary services for a primitive native tribe. In the course of these travels she became aware that there was a band of Franciscan monks already preaching in another part of Mexico and she directed her converts to make their way to this distant missionary settlement. It is said that they did go to the Franciscans for baptism, and told them of the woman in strange garb who had sent them. On being shown a portrait of another Franciscan nun, they at once recognized the habit as identical with that of their visitor from afar who had mysteriously appeared to them so often.

Thurston says that Sister Maria at first said little or nothing of these voyages beyond the seas because she was filled with misgivings, fearing that they were hallucinations. "It happened, however, that she remembered that on one of her journeys she had distributed a number of rosaries to her Indians. Later on, when she came to look for the supply of these chaplets which she kept in her cell, she found that not one was left."

Thurston adds that there purports to be independent evidence attesting the belief of the natives that a woman had come to them from afar. In 1630 Father Alonzo de Benavides, who was then in charge of the mission of New Mexico, was summoned back to Europe. He is said to have brought with him a strange story of a Mexican tribe of Indians who declared that they had been visited and instructed by an unknown woman who bade them seek baptism. Father Benavides was directed by his superiors to visit Maria at Agreda and we are told that he satisfied himself that she was in truth the woman concerned.

10

Mediums

IT WOULD APPEAR THAT PSYCHIC INDIVIDUALS ARE MORE ABLE than others to have astral projections, and also to see those who are having them. Many more people are psychic than realize it, of course. Perhaps they only discover it at some crucial moment, or they may suspect it in their daily sensitivity to the thoughts of others. A psychic whose powers are more consistently at a high point is called a medium.

It can safely be said, reviewing the records, that persons having recurrent out-of-body experiences tend to travel to the kind of places they would expect to visit. Most mediums, who think of themselves as connecting links between this life and the next, usually tell us of visits to spirit land and of meetings with deceased personages.

One does not hear of Eileen Garrett travelling to such places; probably because her approach to the entire subject of parapsychology is critical and with a certain academic objectivity. Sylvan Muldoon, the most habitual astral traveller of them all, strangely enough wrote that he had never had an occasion in which he visited on a higher plane of existence, although he believes very firmly that such planes are a reality. Many other projectors claim to have only the most mundane treatment when out of the body.

Yet some persons report such outrageously unbelievable escapades that it is difficult to take them seriously. Is it, however, fair for us to accept only those accounts which sound as though they could be true, and reject those which seem too incredibly ingenuous? If anything in this book can be accepted as recording actual astral outings, then all of the rest is just as apt to be factual. Are we justified in saying that an astral flight is authentic if it brings back clairvoyant data, and hallucinatory if it merely seems to romanticize about future planes of existence and conditions after death? Some who have done the highest flying in what seem to be worlds of fantasy, have also produced authentic evidence on other occasions.

Gladys Osborne Leonard, one of the greatest mediums the world has ever known, is the most levelheaded of women. Her life has been a model of propriety at all times. During a period of fifty years she was investigated constantly by members of the Society for Psychical Research and never once found to have done anything which might arouse suspicion of dishonesty, or, for that matter, of silliness or instability. Yet Mrs. Leonard says that during astral expeditions she has frequently visited the spirit world, where she has had charming chats with her deceased husband.

Her first encounter with this curious phenomenon, however, brought her information which was completely verifiable, as she has reported in detail in her book *My Life in Two Worlds.* One afternoon early in her married life and shortly after her mediumship had developed, she was resting in her partly darkened room when she felt a strange sensation of being lifted above the bed. She became alert and interested and a little excited, and immediately the feeling of floating in the air left her. (We've been told this before, that mental alertness counteracts the condition necessary for astral orbiting.)

For some weeks after that, Mrs. Leonard says, "I always lay down in a state of expectancy and mental alertness, hoping for a repetition of the experience, but was disappointed, and at length I gave up hope of having any similar manifestation."

One afternoon some weeks later Gladys was expecting a lady and a gentleman for a sitting in which they looked forward to having further communication with their deceased son Philip. She knew very little about these people, who lived many miles from London. Before they came she lay down to rest, feeling a little sleepy. Suddenly the sleepiness vanished and gave way to a calm, then a sort of thrill as if a slight electric current were passing through her body, and again she had the sensation of rising into the air. This time she held her mind under quiet control, and she began an aerial excursion.

First, she became aware of the sound of her husband opening the door to their flat and speaking to someone in the hall outside in a low voice so as not to disturb her. She thought, "I should like to go and see to whom he is speaking," and immediately she was standing at her husband's elbow. The guest was no one more interesting than the man from the gas company.

She says, "What they were talking about I did not notice, because just after I joined them (in my astral body) a maid from one of the upstairs flats passed them, and I saw my husband, without speaking to her, take a coin from his pocket and hand it to her. I thought, 'That's funny. Why did he give that servant a coin?'"

Making a mental note to ask him about it, she began to think of new worlds to conquer, and she went on a tour, which somehow was not consciously directed. She found herself in a room she had never seen before, where the lady and gentleman she was expecting that afternoon were talking to another man, a stranger to her. She heard them ask him to accompany them to the sitting at Mrs. Leonard's.

Next, after a period of confusion as to just where she was, she saw Philip, the deceased son of her sitters. She recognized him because at one of their previous séances she had seen him clairvoyantly and described him to his parents. She asked him who it was she could hear playing the piano and singing and he said it was his cousin Gertrude. He said she used to come and play and sing for him every week before they both had died, and that she now continued the practice in the spirit world.

Gladys went with Philip into a room where the young lady was sitting at a grand piano. She memorized the details of the girl's appearance and the room so that she could use them for verification when her sitters arrived, for she had begun to realize that what was happening was probably intended to give her evidence for them. Soon her mind became hazy, and then she found herself at home, hovering over her body on the bed.

After she was safely back, Gladys rushed to notify her husband. He was exceedingly skeptical until told about giving the servant the coin, which he said was for a trifling service she had done a few days before when he did not happen to have any change. Gladys also described for him the man who was going to accompany her sitters that afternoon.

The gentleman did arrive, and was the lady's brother. And when she checked she learned that Cousin Gertrude was really the girl she had seen and that she had come once a week to play and sing for Philip in a room answering the description of the one where Gladys had seen her. The sitters and everyone involved were entranced with the evidence produced by Gladys Leonard's first out-of-body experience.

A New York City medium, Betty Ritter, tells me that such things happen to her while she is in the trance state. When she holds a séance she sits in a corner of her room which has been partitioned off with a dark curtain to make a cabinet. Then she seems to go to sleep, but she says she actually goes into a dead trance, in which travelling clairvoyance occurs.

The late L. C. Andrews, who was doing some experiments for the American Society for Psychical Research, came to her séance one night carrying a securely wrapped and tied package somewhat larger than a shoe box, whose contents he himself did not even know. Betty attempted to learn supernormally what the box contained. When she had attained the dead trance state, she found herself standing in a deep, dark place somewhere in Egypt. She saw two men who looked like priests carrying a box. "There were mummies all around," Betty Ritter recalls.

When she came out of her trance she gave Mr. Andrews the message that the box contained a mummy from Egypt. She also told him certain letters of the alphabet which had a special significance, but she did not know exactly what they meant. When the box was opened it was found to contain a small carved mummy case. The letters she had mentioned were cut into the base of it as if to identify the man who had carved it. The little sarcophagus was stamped, "Made in Egypt."

Sophia Williams, probably the greatest direct voice medium of recent times, has described the trance state in her book *You Are Psychic*: "During the period of trance, while the body of the medium sits, or lies quietly asleep . . . the ego or *actual self of the medium* may travel, see other places, visit someone at a distance who will be quite unaware of his or her presence, and even visit and talk with those who have ostensibly died. One may travel to a distant place, enter the home of a friend, note the exact time by clock, describe the room and other details, and afterwards verify each detail of the trip.

"In contrast to our movements while awake, this travel is effortless. For instance, I might desire to go from Chicago to New York while in trance. I seem to be there instantly, without the sensation of having travelled at all. It is thought travel and yet one actually goes, sees things he has never seen before and can later give accurate descriptions of the places he visits. Thoughts are definite things and we must learn to objectify our thoughts by putting them into action. We do this when we desire to perform astral travel. Before going into trance we plan a trip we wish to make, and then set about making it without any physical activity whatsoever. . . .

"The thing which hampers us most is that *we cannot think of ourselves apart from our physical bodies*, but in a state of trance we are oblivious to the physical part of us, and the ego or self, being unobstructed, acts with freedom."

As a developing medium grows in power, a man named Henry S. Hillers says, it is possible for him to acquire this ability to have an out-of-body experience, and even to learn to make himself seen. In an article entitled "Projecting the Etheric Body" in the *Journal* of the American Society for Psychical Research, Hillers speaks of various pupils who had acquired this power to some extent or other. Of Case No. 3 he writes: "This subject had sat in spiritualistic classes for the purpose of developing materialization. At the sixth sitting I was able to loosen up the etheric and she experienced a sensation of floating. After some effort I uprighted her about five feet from her physical body. All observers noted a luminous-like smoke in the same location that her etheric body was supposed to be. Flashing-like points of light condensation continued in this luminous cloud for about twenty minutes.

"At the second sitting I suggested that she try materialization, and in about ten minutes we were rewarded by seeing this white cloud-like substance assume the exact reproduction of her face. The lady refused further sittings and went back to attend her spiritual classes."

Hillers says, "I maintain that a person who succeeds in projecting independently can do so only through a process of self-hypnotization."

But mediums can have out-of-body experiences without going into any kind of trance at all. Mrs. Willett (the pseudonym under which the highly sensitive Mrs. Winifred Coombe-Tennant worked) is called an autonomist, because she received communications purporting to come from the spirit world while in a "withdrawn" or "mentally dissociated" state. She did not go into trance. Yet she seems to have achieved some kind of an out-of-body condition, for she said at the conclusion of a sitting, "It's just like waking up in prison from a dream that one has been at home. Don't you ever walk out of yourself? Aren't you tired of being always yourself? It's so heavenly to be out of myself—when I am everything, and everything else is me."

Another famous medium of the past, the Reverend Stainton Moses, was an Oxford graduate, a clergyman of the Church of England, and by occupation a teacher. At the request of Edmund Gurney, who was compiling the material for *Phantasms of the Living*, Moses wrote of an experience of his own, when he resolved to try to appear to a friend at some distance. He did not warn him beforehand. When he retired his thoughts were fixed upon his friend, but he soon fell asleep and awoke the next morning unconscious that anything had taken place.

The next time he saw his friend, however, he was told, "I had been sitting over the fire with M., smoking and chatting. About 12:30 he rose to leave. . . . I returned to the fire to finish my pipe when I saw you sitting in the chair just vacated by him. . . . While I gazed without speaking, you faded away."

Moses said, "The next time I come, ask me what I want, as I had fixed on my mind certain questions I intended to ask you, but I was probably waiting for an invitation to speak."

A few weeks later the experiment was repeated with equal success, but on this occasion the friend not only questioned Moses on a subject which was at that time under very warm discussion between them, but detained him by the exercise of his will some time after Moses had intimated a desire to leave. It is to this fact that the Reverend Stainton Moses attributed the headache which he had on the morning following the experiment.

Roy Eugene Davis, author and lecturer on metaphysics, was for several years a disciple of the late Yoga teacher Paramahansa Yogananda. Davis has had an occasional out-of-body experience while awake; and during sleep he has dreamed vividly, clearly, and in color for many years. But he is most curious about the dream-visions which have occurred since Yogananda's passing. There are certain times at night when he is quite sure that he and his brother disciples meet with Yogananda and receive instruction from him.

Davis did not know whether to classify this experience as a dream or an astral projection into the spirit world until he discussed it with his fellow disciple, Daniel Boone of Yucca Valley, California. Boone revealed to him that he also has similar impressions of meeting with Yogananda and the others.

A letter from Boone confirms Davis's story. He writes, "Yes, I have had similar experiences to those of my brother-disciple, Roy Davis." Boone adds, "Who is to say they are not actual astral experiences?" He admits that it is difficult for one who has not had first-hand repeated astral travel to distinguish it from a vivid dream. "However," he adds, "the Yogins know ways to produce both, and to tell the difference."

Boone has had many other out-of-body experiences, but they were most often in the astral planes and so he does not feel that they have any evidential value. Their teacher Yogananda has said, "Thousands of earth-dwellers have momentarily glimpsed an astral being or an astral world." That his pupils should be convinced they have done so is not surprising.

Many people think that some of the greatest saints were actually mediumistic and that their mystical powers were really psychic. St. Teresa d'Avila, for instance, once wrote, "I was so raised up in spirit that I thought myself to be, as it were, out of the body; at least, I did not know that I was living in it. I had a vision of the most Sacred Humanity in exceeding glory, greater than I had ever seen It in before. . . ."

And again, St. Teresa wrote: "I was rapt in spirit with such violence that I could make no resistance whatever. It seemed to me that I was taken up to heaven; and the first persons I saw there were my father and my mother."

St. Paul would have agreed heartily that this is an actual out-of-body experience, according to his statement about a similar incident. In II Corinthians, 12.2, St. Paul writes:

"I know a man in Christ, fourteen years ago (whether in the body, I know not; or whether out of the body, I know not; God knoweth), such a one caught up even to the third heaven.

And I know such a man (whether in the body, or apart from the body, I know not; God knoweth), how that he was caught up into Paradise, and heard unspeakable words, which it is not lawful for a man to utter."

St. Paul believed that these were "visions and revelations of the Lord."

But persons with mediumistic powers have similar visions and revelations—whether from On High or not, who knoweth? Harriett M. Shelton, a clairvoyant, is an example. She tells me that from practice she has developed to the point that she can have out-of-body experiences almost any time she wishes.

Although most of her projections bring no more evidence than the stories told by other travellers to the spirit worlds, Miss Shelton has had one reciprocal occurrence for which I have been able to acquire the testimony of witnesses.

On the nights when the Reverends Kenneth and Gladys Custance hold meetings in Onset, Massachusetts, Miss Shelton in her New York apartment sometimes attempts to visit them by astral projection. The first time she made such an effort was a Friday in March, 1963. No one at the Onset meeting knew that she had them in mind or that she was attempting to be seen by them. None of the group was talking about her at the time, nor had her name been mentioned earlier. Suddenly Meroë Morse and Kay Detrich spoke up at the same time, saying, "There's Miss Shelton." They actually saw her phantom.

And so with this corroborative testimony that she does have legitimate out-of-body experiences, let us now visit her "Summerland" with Miss Shelton as our guide. She first bandages her eyes, and soon finds herself walking on a road of moss down a long tunnel made of overhanging trees.

"For a long time," she says in a little booklet called *Astral Flights*, "it was difficult for me to believe that my etheric body was floating along some ethereal country road very like those you see in Connecticut or Massachusetts. On the planes I have visited, the dirt roads wind along, up and down through wooded areas where the trees meet overhead. There are roadside flowers which are more vivid in color than ours, and I am told that they never fade. Birds flit from tree to tree, and an occasional rabbit crosses the road ahead. Now and then a house by the roadside seems to be a replica of some much-loved home on earth. My father's astral country place is almost an exact copy of one he had in Ridgefield."

Miss Shelton says she has visited often with her parents and her deceased husband. She has also had audiences with venerable figures of the past in higher planes of the spirit world, where the palace of Buddha, for instance, built of gold and covered with precious gems, is so spectacularly gorgeous that words fail her in attempting to describe it.

Among the most charming of Miss Shelton's tales are her visits with children in their after-death world: "For those who have lost a child I hope my description of these thousands of little ones playing and laughing as children do, will comfort them," she says. The children play on grassy bowers and run and splash in the water, with no one having to tell them, "Don't do this, it's dangerous," or "Stop that, you'll get hurt." The more adventurous were diving in and out of a lake and playing under a waterfall. She writes: "As I stood watching them, I saw a number of boys running along the shore. They appeared to be in great excitement, and I realized that they were having a race. You will never believe me when I tell you that porpoises were leaping along through the water with small boys clinging to their backs. . . . Then, out of the woods, to my astonishment, hopped two enormous bright green frogs with small boys riding them."

The most enchanting of Miss Shelton's stories, as well as the one that takes the greatest credulity to believe, occurred when she was spending a recent summer in Onset. She was sitting one afternoon with Gladys Custance, when she went into trance and was taken to visit the Animal Kingdom. There, after other encounters with animal life she noticed a handsome black-maned lion walking slowly toward her. She asked her guide, whom she calls "the professor," if it would be safe to touch him.

"Speak to him first, and see how he responds," was the answer. This was unnecessary as the lion came up to her and rubbed his head against her knees. Just then on the earth plane Gladys Custance's large black dog, Rastus, burst through the door of the room in which the two ladies were sitting, and flopped down on the floor in front of his mistress' feet.

Miss Shelton writes: "The lion now looked up, saw Rastus, and walked over to him. Just then Rastus saw the lion; he let out a wild yelp and tore out of the room and down the stairs as fast as he could go. I could never get him to come up into my apartment again.

"Many people have asked me how Rastus, who was in Onset, and the lion, who was in the Celestial Animal Kingdom, could see each other. I asked the professor about this. He explained that animals are more psychic than people and can tune in to certain vibrations which are present, under just the right conditions."

Whatever these conditions are, they should be encouraged by all concerned. Life couldn't help but be sweeter in a land where a lion acts just like a big old pussy-cat.

II

Children and Primitives

THAT FAR-OUT WORLDS ARE MORE ACCESSIBLE TO CHILDREN THAN adults is a recognized fact. Not having the inhibitions that adults have been forced by the vicissitudes of life to acquire, children quite frequently accept psychic experiences as natural, until adults scare or scold it out of them.

Yet where the child's imagination leaves off and a genuine psychic event begins is difficult to determine. Let us try with two out-of-body stories which have a ring of authenticity. They were received from two little girls by Samuel Silverstein of Torrington, Connecticut. A very perceptive teacher, Silverstein was at that time conducting a "creative expression" class in a grammar school.

Silverstein asked the children to attempt to interpret any strange feelings or occurrences they had by drawing pictures illustrating what happened, and then to explain the pictures to him. He assures me that he was very careful not to suggest any ideas to them, but only to listen to the stories, extracting them by careful questioning. He says:

It was during the last period of the day that D.E. brought a drawing up to my desk and said, "This is what I saw happen to me Sunday in church."

"Do you want to explain your drawing?" I asked.

D.E. said that it was after saying a prayer that she felt sort of light and then she was able to see herself float up to the ceiling.

Then from the sky there came a red line circling down and headed toward her as she floated there.

"The line came in near the shoulder," D.E. said, "and went down to the heart. I could see the heart and it was giving off a red light. When the line touched the heart, the heart turned to a yellow glow, and red wiggly lines started to spread out inside the body, filling it almost full."

The golden glow then filled up the rest of her body and it also moved out a short distance, and then she realized that her whole body was surrounded by the yellow light. At this time a feeling of great happiness swept through her. As this eight-year-old child was telling of her happy feeling, her voice lowered to a whisper and then stopped. I looked up from her drawing on the desk and saw her staring off into space with a look of peaceful joy upon her face. After a while she started talking again, and I asked her what had just occurred.

"As I was telling you what happened in church," D.E. said, "some of that nice feeling came back to me all over again."

"Was there anything else that you could remember? What are these lines here coming out from the body?" I asked, pointing to her drawing on the desk.

"Oh, that," she said, "that was a wind of some sort . . . like air rushing out . . . but that came afterwards."

"Where did the wind come from?"

"I don't know," D.E. said, "but when I felt the happiness go through me, I started to feel something in me trying to push out of me . . . if you know what I mean . . . but it couldn't get out."

"So what happened next?"

"Well, the happy feeling lasted a long time. Then the wind started to come out from my legs. Then it came out of both hands, and then my head. After that there wasn't any more air rushing out, and the feeling of something inside of me pushing out was gone . . . and the happiness was gone too."

The second out-of-body case reported by Samuel Silverstein is just as interesting:

J.S. came up to my desk one day after school with a drawing in her hand.

"I have a picture I want to show you," she said. During the last period of the day, which was a creative expression period,

J.S. did not have an opportunity to tell the thing that had happened to her the night before, so she stayed after school when there was more time to talk. Her drawing looked interesting and I asked her what it represented.

"Last night while I was in bed it happened," J.S. said. "I was sort of half-awake and half-asleep when up in the sky I was able to see a blue wave like come down and it came right towards me and went into my body."

"How did it get into your body?" I asked.

"It came in to my head first. Then it went down one side, going into the right arm, then down to the right leg, then over to the other side, to the left foot, up to the left arm, and then back up to the head."

"How could you tell what was happening?" I asked.

"I felt the line doing that. And I could see it."

"Do you mean you could see the line moving like that inside your body?"

"That's right," J.S. said. "I could see inside my body."

J. S. went on with a good bit more description of flashes of light and other strange things which were happening inside her, and then she said:

"The next thing I knew I felt myself floating up towards the ceiling, and I looked down, and there was my body still lying in bed."

"What happened next?" I asked.

"Next," J.S. said, "I seemed to go right through the ceiling, through the roof of the house, and out into the night. And I went to different places. One place I went to was the house of my friend. I saw her in the house, but she couldn't see me. And pretty soon I left . . . and that's all there was that happened."

The teacher adds that "The children in much of their talking about their experiences, kept telling of religious actions. They told of a place up in the sky that they travel to that they call heaven. They talk about the people they meet from there."

Heaven is always in the sky, and everyone always wants to go to heaven. We know that there is a universal unconscious wish in every one of us to fly. Children unable to read and isolated aborigines use the same analogies and desire the same goals. Folklore about this among primitive peoples is entirely similar, and the tradition that shamans, heroes, sovereigns, and initiates can reach the sky in one way or another is world-wide. The myth of ascent to the sky by ladder comes from alchemical tradition as well as Biblical. It is also known among the primitives of Africa, Oceania, and North America. The sky may be reached by fire or smoke, by climbing stairs, or a tree or a mountain, or ascending by way of a rope or vine, or the rainbow, or even a sunbeam, or by becoming a bird.

This general concept is perfectly normal, and I understand it. What I don't understand is how these two little girls knew about leaving their bodies and how the one looked back down at hers lying on the bed—exactly as adults have described it—unless they, themselves, also experienced it. Mr. Silverstein assures us that no other members of the class ever reported any such incidents, and none of them had discussed anything of this nature. It is certainly not the kind of thing the girls would have learned at their mother's knee.

It was called to my attention by a psychical researcher that it would be interesting to compare what can be learned about the experiences of preliterate people with the present-day records. "You will not find the modern out-of-the-body type among the former," he said. And so it was with the feeling that my search would probably be unfruitful that I began to peruse books about primitives.

Oddly enough, what I discovered seemed to me to indicate just the opposite. Naturally, an aborigine is not going to state his experiences in identical, or even similar, terminology to that used by the literate person. And naturally magic enters into his thinking about what is happening to him. Like children, primitives take the supernormal for granted. But buried among their magic, omens, totems, self-delusions, and hocus-pocus there are recurrent themes entirely similar to our out-of-body experiences. For instance:

We learn from Mircea Eliade in *Shamanism: Archaic Techniques of Ecstasy* that the shamans or high-priests of primitive cultures are especially trained in ways to experience ecstasy. The shaman brings on trance by the use of such mechanical means as narcotics, dancing to the point of exhaustion, etc., and then he visits the underworld, heaven, the shores of the nine seas, or wherever else he wants to go, and he has impressions which are comparable to those of our mediums.

Among the powers of the medicine man of the Mara tribe is that of climbing at night by means of a rope invisible to ordinary mortals into the sky, where he can hold converse with the star people. Shamans of the Dyak tribe of Borneo have an ecstatic journey to the sky on a ritual ladder. A great prophet in Basutoland, British South Africa, received his vocation after an ecstasy during which he saw the roof of his hut open above his head and felt himself carried off to the sky, where he met a multitude of spirits. A Baffinland Eskimo shaman was carried to the moon and after many adventures returned to his body, which had remained inanimate during his ecstasy.

In ancient Greek mythology Aristaeus of Proconnesus fell into ecstasy and the god Apollo seized his soul; then he could appear at the same time in places far apart. Hermotimos of Clazomenae had the power of leaving his body for many years, during which he journeyed to great distances and brought back much mantic lore and knowledge of the future. The Ancient Chinese had magicians whose primary art consisted in exteriorizing their souls and journeying in spirit. Eliade says, "All these mythological and folklore traditions have their point of departure in an ideology and technique of ecstasy that imply journeying in spirit."

Among the Iglulik Eskimos the initiation of the shaman begins with an operation in which the old *angakok* extracts the disciple's "soul" from his eyes, brain and intestines, so that the spirits may know what is best in him. After this extraction of the soul the future shaman himself becomes able to draw his soul from his body and undertake long mystical journeys through space and the depths of the sea.

Ceremonies are common among the Eskimos in which, being lashed from head to foot, the shaman sets free his soul and travels through the air, finally returning to his body and releasing it from its bonds. Peter Freuchen, author of *The Book of the Eskimos*, even believed that he saw the physical body of a shaman disappear for a time, while tightly bound and in plain view of all the assembled Eskimos and himself.

But aside from the high priests and magicians, whose assertions of astral flights may, at least on most occasions, be symbolic—what about the ordinary people of these primitive cultures? They have the same ordinary, everyday, run-of-the-mill, out-of-the-body experiences that our ordinary people do. Here is a typical instance:

In New Zealand, an old Maori woman who lived near Rotorua some years ago was taken ill and died, according to the belief of her relatives, who laid her out in native fashion and then left her. Two days later two natives were paddling along the coast in their canoe when the old woman called to them. She told of having travelled to the spirit world with one of her deceased relatives. She arrived at a village where there were several of her acquaintances who had died previously. They offered her food, but the relative told her not to take any or she would never be able to return to earth. After numerous adventures she was told she had to care for this relative's grandchildren on earth and so must come alive again. And so she did. Just as our Mrs. Ruopp did after looking through the window of heaven and watching the little children playing.

It is somehow to be doubted that this old Maori woman had read Muldoon or Oliver Fox. Where did she get her information about leaving the body and visiting the spirit realms? Perhaps, in her culture, it *was* at her mother's knee.

John Slocum of Puget Sound, a prophet in the Ghost-Dance religion, died and saw his soul leave his body. He said to an anthropologist who was making notes about authentic Indian experiences, "All at once I saw a shining light—a great light—I looked and saw my body had no soul—looked at my own body—it was dead. My soul left my body and went up to the judgment place of God."

Here is the tale of a Hopi Indian lad named Don, in his middle teens in 1907 when he was attending the Sherman Indian School in Riverside, California. He became quite ill with pneumonia, and on Christmas Eve he shut his eyes and appeared to have died. A spirit came to take him to see the place where the dead people are, according to his later account. He walked down the hospital stairs as if he were treading on air and soon reached the San Bernardino mountains. He climbed halfway up until he saw a tunnel within which there was a sort of foggy light. He went through it and then visited his ancestors and had many conversations with them. He was finally told by his ancient relatives, "Now you have seen what you wanted to see. Now go back, and be careful, thoughtful, wise and good. . . ."

In his vision Don then ran back to the mountain, through the tunnel, down the mountain and into the hospital. He opened his eyes in bed and the nurses sitting beside him said, "Well, my boy, you've come to life." They had washed his face and combed his hair and were almost ready to put him in a coffin. Don asked for food, saying he was hungry after his travel, but the nurses told him, "You didn't travel, you stayed right here."

Now, I'm not maintaining that Don actually did travel, even out-of-his-body. He could have had an hallucination. But he certainly had a story to tell that was strangely like those we are reading about today among people of a higher cultural level.

Ronald Rose and his wife spent a long time among the Australian aborigines studying them in detail. Rose then published his findings in *Living Magic*. In it he writes:

"Although he would joke about most aspects of his people's magical ideas, even bone pointing, there was one aspect that

Tjalkalieri always discussed with the utmost gravity, although, on the face of it, it was a wildly improbable notion. This was the belief, widely held, that doctors could travel vast distances in a short time with the aid of their magic cords.

"Frequently he mentioned that Winjin or some other clever-man he knew could perform such miracles. Often on a journey he would say, 'We take two day, three day, but that Winjin fellow, he can travel in no time.'

"Similarly, coastal natives believed in this ability to travel fast that so closely resembles the claims of Yogi of Tibet. There is evidence, too, that in a sort of trance state a native might become aware of events at a distance as though he had actually travelled there. Technically this is known as 'travelling clairvoyance.' There is no doubt that natives believe they actually experience this.

"Old Fred Cowlin told me he could travel thus from northern New South Wales to Brisbane. He could not, however, travel to Sydney. He said it was too far.

"The son of a clever-man told me he had seen his father go to a creek, take off his clothes, and disappear. When he reappeared, only a few minutes later, he would claim to have travelled some hundreds of miles, and would give an account of what he had seen, which was often confirmed later."

And so these primitive people have experiences which follow a pattern—and it is the same pattern we have found to exist among the rest of us.

12

Ecstatic
States

HAVING JUST MET A GROUP WHO INSTINCTIVELY HAVE AN UN-
critical acceptance of astral projection as quite proper and
ordinary, we may now find it easier to understand Dr. Robert
Crookall's statement that leaving the body is a natural and
not an abnormal process. Crookall also says that four out of
every five cases of temporary exteriorization concern people
who are normal and well. "This proportion," he adds, "is the
more remarkable in view of the fact that illness and pain are
among the causes of exteriorization."

Actually, in times of extreme pain it would appear that the
best possible relief is an out-of-body exodus. George Jones says
that when a period of severe pain occurs to him, he deliberately
projects his consciousness away from his body in order to
escape it. Once when in an automobile accident, he left his
body at the moment of impact. He suffered no shock and very
little physical damage, and was able to continue driving shortly
afterward with no ill effects.

Something similar occurred spontaneously to a distinguished
mountaineer named F. S. Smythe, who told of it in *The Spirit
of the Hills*. He and a friend were climbing in the Dolomites
when there was a sudden crash of falling rock. He found himself, with his climbing rope attached, plunging down the
mountainside. Sliding and bumping along, he turned first on
his side, then on his back, driving his heels, elbows, forearms

and the palms of his hands against the rocks in an endeavor to stop himself. For ten or twelve feet he thus slid, then shot over the edge of a precipice, where he hung by the rope a few feet below the crest of the ridge. He snatched at the rocks and clawed his way back to safety, discovering that altogether he had fallen about twenty feet.

Smythe had been sure with half his mind that he would be killed; nevertheless he had made the desperate attempts to stop himself.

"During the time that I was doing this," he writes, "a curious rigidity or tension gripped my whole mental and physical being. So great was this tension that it swamped all pain and fear, and rendered me insensible to bumps and blows." It was an overwhelming sensation, quite outside his previous experience. Then, suddenly, this feeling was superseded by one of complete indifference to what happened to his body, detachment from what was happening or likely to happen to it.

"I seemed to stand aside from my body," he writes. "I was not falling, for the reason that I was not in a dimension where it was possible to fall. I, that is my consciousness, was apart from my body, and not in the least concerned with what was befalling it. My body was in the process of being injured, crushed and pulped, and my consciousness was not associated with these physical injuries, and was completely uninterested in them. Had the tenant already departed in anticipation of the wreck that was to follow? Had the assumption of death—when my slide was not checked by the rope I assumed death as certain—resulted in a partial effect due to a sudden and intense nervous strain? It is not within my province to discuss that which only death can prove; yet to me this experience was a convincing one; it convinced me that consciousness survives beyond the grave."

Smythe's final conclusion about his whole exhausting effort: "I know now that death is not to be feared, it is a supreme experience, the climax, not the anticlimax, of life."

There is no doubt that this book is recording a fantastic number of soul-searing (or soul-revealing?) events. This is because the subject under discussion occurs so frequently at times of crisis. And it does not happen, as most of our material would indicate, only in the nineteenth and twentieth centuries of modern enlightenment. Be assured that the records contain similar instances from ages past. A famous Italian mathematician and physician of the sixteenth century, Girolamo Cardano, began in his fifty-fifth year to experience peculiar ecstatic states during which, he said, "I have near my heart a feeling as though the spirit detached itself from the body, and this separation extends to all the body, especially the head and neck. After that, I have no longer the idea of any sensation, except of feeling myself outside of the body." Because all his sensibilities were exteriorized, during his ecstasies Cardano did not have to endure the pains of gout from which he suffered exceedingly in his normal state.

Such "peculiar ecstatic states" as Cardano's are by no means unusual, although they do not necessarily bring with them out-of-body experiences. Still, etymologically, "ecstasy" is "to stand outside oneself," so don't be surprised if we find an occasional expansion of awareness during ecstasy which corresponds to astral projections.

Ecstatic states can reach such high pinnacles that a feeling of illumination about the divine order of nature is achieved. Many who are illumined become great spiritual leaders, teachers, or artists. Jesus, Gautama (the Buddha), Dante, Jakob Boehme (or Behman), William Blake, and Walt Whitman are but a few of those who have undergone illumination. It is called "cosmic consciousness" by Dr. Richard M. Bucke, who says that it brings with it an intellectual enlightenment which alone would place the individual on a new plane of existence —would make him almost a member of a new species.

Bucke describes illumination, or cosmic consciousness, as "a state of moral exaltation, an indescribable feeling of elevation, elation, and joyousness, and a quickening of the moral sense. . . . With these come what may be called a sense of immortality, a consciousness of eternal life, not a conviction that he shall have this, but the consciousness that he has it already."

A description of an ecstatic vision or moment of illumination is given by Paramahansa Yogananda in *Autobiography of a Yogi*. He says that suddenly,

> My body became immovably rooted; breath was drawn out of my lungs as if by some huge magnet. Soul and mind instantly lost their physical bondage, and streamed out like a fluid piercing light from my every pore. The flesh was as though dead, yet in my intense awareness I knew that never before had I been fully alive. My sense of identity was no longer narrowly confined to a body, but embraced the circumambient atoms. . . .
>
> The whole vicinity lay bare before me. My ordinary frontal vision was now changed to a vast spherical sight, simultaneously all-perceptive. . . .
>
> A swelling glory within me began to envelop towns, continents, the earth, solar and stellar systems, tenuous nebulae, and floating universes. The entire cosmos, gently luminous, like a city seen afar at night, glimmering within the infinitude of my being. . . ."

Eventually the breath returned to his lungs. With a disappointment almost unbearable, he realized that his infinite immensity was lost. "Once more," he says, "I was limited to the humiliating cage of a body, not easily accommodative ·to the Spirit."

It would seem here that in his ecstatic state Yogananda's consciousness had expanded to take in more than his normal vision, more than his normal perceptions, and considerably more than his normal understanding. Emanuel Swedenborg exemplified this type of illumination, and added another dimension to it, for when his awareness expanded it caused him to be sure that he was functioning in two areas of existence simultaneously. He wrote books about his visions of the spirit planes, reporting on conditions as he saw them. His explorations remind us very much of those of the mediums who, when having astral projections, envision themselves as visiting in other worlds.

Now this expansion of consciousness or expansion of awareness is a concept which keeps creeping into our attention from a variety of sources. Perhaps it can be accepted, at least for now, as the definition of one form of out-of-body experience—one in which only the mind is projected without the accompaniment of the astral body.

Certain new drugs, called hallucinogens, or psychedelics, sometimes produce this expansion of awareness in the individuals who indulge in them. On occasion by this artificial manner a condition close to ecstasy is attained. The use of these psychedelic drugs is not recommended unless they are taken under the supervision of a physician familiar with them, primarily because they have not been tested enough for their full effect to be known. They may produce schizophrenic conditions, even to the point of possible permanent damage, according to some authorities. However, others who have used psychedelics under proper control have had remarkable results.

Jane Dunlap, a pseudonym for a well-known nutritionist, writes in *Exploring Inner Space* of her ecstatic as well as startling visions after taking LSD—lysergic acid diethylamide. Opening her book at random, one finds on page 187:

"Suddenly a great beam of light focused on me, and against a background of darkness I became an exploding atomic bomb which tore my body asunder yet showed me unutterable beauty . . . While I watched a universe aglitter with fountains of falling sparks, I knew I had been given some small insight of the strength upon which God's peace was built."

She also says later:

"Then, as during and after every experience, my mind turned in awe and amazement to wondering where such insights and overpowering emotions could come from. I thought of how persons who had not taken the drug argued that such material must originate entirely in the subject's own background, understanding, knowledge, yearnings, and conflicts, pointing out that anyone ignorant of evolution could not have lived it as I had. Individuals who had been highly rewarded by LSD invariably argued with equal vigor that material unrelated to one's life experience did at times present itself. Certainly the many convictions, feelings, and insights I had had this day had not come from my past; and every experience had caused me to run to the encyclopedia to check the accuracy of material. . . . Unrecognized sources of wisdom did seem to be set free by the drug."

Expansion of consciousness to incorporate all things, as we have suggested?

Out-of-body experiences are not uncommon when taking LSD. A prominent New York City psychologist writes me of his own experience in this regard on July 29, 1957:

"I felt as if I were almost completely detached from my physical body. My physical body was just a dead weight that I was aware of, as if I were looking down on it from a great height. The experience was one of height and light. . . . I seemed to be a pinpoint in space—space all around me in every dimension, space filled with light, not a blinding light but a radiant light—and space that was not just empty space, but space pregnant with meaning—a meaning that I couldn't comprehend but which I felt very distinctly—space that was peopled, perhaps, with some knowing force."

The doctor goes on that the outstanding characteristic of this drug state is the clarity of the mind. "When I say the mind I mean certainly the higher mind, the 'I' in capitals. It was this 'I,' this most real part of the Me which I felt soared on this flight . . . utterly awake, utterly sensitive, far more sensitive than in the usual state to forces around me and certainly beyond the spectrum which I in the usual waking state could be aware of. Certainly I brought back from this experience an even greater conviction of the preservation of this 'I' beyond that thing which we call physical death. I felt so completely separate from and so distinct from my physical self that it would seem utterly incomprehensible or illogical that this 'I' should become extinct when this worn out carcass of mine gives up in the end."

13

The
Psychic Ether

THERE IS NO REASON TO SUPPOSE, IN ATTEMPTING TO UNDERSTAND out-of-body experiences, that any one answer is the only answer. The concept of astral projection is bound to include as many causes as it does varieties of expression. Nothing in nature is simple, everything has many facets, many aspects, and often multiple reasons. So when reaching for an explanation to anything as complex as this, which involves so many obviously little-known or unknown laws, we must leave ourselves wide open to new ideas.

It would appear from the case histories so far presented that the astral body may travel out of the physical body and be accompanied by the conscious mind, which retains memories of the trip and (sometimes) of information it has gleaned. But the astral body may also leave while the mental capacities remain with the physical body. This is then an apparition of the living, or even a doppelgänger, which may be seen by the individual himself.

In the chapter on ecstasy we had to do with what appears to be merely a mental event—but what an event! When the powers of awareness are expanded so wide as to encompass the great truths of life, illumination or cosmic consciousness is experienced. An expansion of awareness in which information is acquired is called psychic, for the perception occurs in an extrasensory, or supernormal, manner. Expansion of awareness may be considered to be a form of out-of-body experience when the individual believes himself to be travelling in spirit planes of existence.

We also have to consider some very peculiar circumstances which are general to all these types of projections. The matter of clothing, for instance. When seen, astral travellers are usually dressed. Oliver Fox has observed his body seemingly clothed in many ways, but never naked except once. In the mirror, Gerhardi saw himself in his pajamas just as he had gone to bed. Rosalind Heywood's other self appeared in a white Madonna-like veil; J. Hewat McKenzie wore a "teddy-bear" woollen overcoat when Mrs. Hankey saw him.

To make the whole thing even more confusing, Fox has also written, "Occasionally I have not been able to see any astral body when I looked for it—no legs, no arms, no body!—an extraordinary sensation—just a *consciousness*, a man invisible even to himself, passing through busy streets or whizzing through space."

Trying to solve these problems is now going to lead us into another highly controversial area—but one which has to be dealt with—the power of thought.

Hasketh Zerla, author of A *Logical Assumption*, says: "You will find that the power of thought is the greatest power in the world. The identity and the description of an exteriorized individual is established by his own awareness of himself. He does not have to think, 'My eyes are blue, my hair is blonde, I am wearing a brown suit.' His conscious awareness of himself as an entity is enough. It is more like a physical process than a mental one, because particularly on the astral plane, where its proper use is understood, thought is a potent force."

Muldoon thoroughly agrees: "It is thought which sustains the astral body," he says. "Do you think that the astral phantom walks upon the floor of a house because the floor holds him up? NO! Never that! He is independent of the floor; he does not make contact with the floor at all. Yet he can walk upon it! Why? Merely because his thought sustains him. He has always walked upon floors in the physical, and, through force of habit, thus learned in the physical—the habit rooted in the subconscious mind—he is sustained. The habit of walking upon a floor permits a phantom to do that in the astral— holds him on the line of the floor. . . . All this can never be explained by mortal mind—how thought creates or makes 'reality' in the astral world."

There are those who say that it is possible for an experimental group of people to concentrate fixedly enough upon an idea to produce an actual picture or reproduction of it, visible to all. Professor Ducasse says in A *Philosophical Scrutiny of Religion:*

"Some support would be lent to the idea—fantastic to us —that a voluntarily created mental image diligently and persistently labored at may acquire in some degree an existence independent of its creator's mind, if we were to accept an experiment which Mme. David-Neel relates she once made to test for herself the assertions to that effect current among the lamas."

Alexandra David-Neel, a French Buddhist who spent years in Tibet and learned many of the practices of the Tibetan Yogis, relates her experiences in her book *With Mystics and Magicians in Tibet.* In it she speaks of the mysterious *tulpa,* an apparition corresponding to some living or imaginary person or deity. It is a visible and sometimes tangible thought-form independent of its creator. Mme. David-Neel says that on more than one occasion she saw such *tulpas* of people known to her which disappeared before her very eyes in broad daylight. Being an expert in the control and concentration of thought she decided to attempt to create a *tulpa* of her own.

In a hermitage she spent some months concentrating on the figure of a stout, short lama, guileless and jovial. She then continued her tour with servants and tents—and the monk went with them. "Now and then," she says, "it was not necessary for me to think of him to make him appear. The phantom performed various actions of the kind that are natural to travellers and that I had not commanded."

But now comes what Ducasse calls the more interesting part: Mme. David-Neel says, "A change gradually took place in my lama. The countenance I had given him altered; his chubby cheeks thinned and his expression became vaguely cunning and malevolent. He became more importunate. In short, he was escaping me. One day a shepherd who was bringing me butter *saw* the phantasm, which he took for a lama of flesh and bone."

The situation, by then, was getting on Mme. David-Neel's nerves, so, she decided to dissipate this creation over which she did not have complete mastery. "I succeeded," she said, "but only after working at it for six months. My lama was hard to kill. That I should have succeeded in obtaining a voluntary hallucination is not surprising. What is interesting in such cases of 'materalization' is that other persons see the form created by thought."

Almost all psychical researchers who go deeply enough into the subject to try to comprehend what is taking place behind all the supernormal phenomena they are observing, have attempted to formulate a theory. Few of them would agree with a concept which would probably seem to them so naïve as "thoughts are things"; but they have arrived at something else which may actually be similar, if we can clarify both concepts enough to compare them. "Psychic ether" (or "aether") is the term some parapsychologists have accepted.

Professor C. D. Broad of Cambridge University has said, "We must consider seriously the possibility that each person's experiences initiate more or less permanent modifications of structure or process in something which is neither his mind nor his brain." This is Broad's academic way of getting at the idea. Now, with the help of Dr. Raynor C. Johnson, we shall attempt to define this substratum which can be modified by thoughts and which seems to be involved in some out-of-body experiences, if not all.

Johnson says in *The Imprisoned Splendour*, "I postulate a psychic aether or 'substance' which partakes of some of the qualities of matter (such as localization in space and retention of form), and which is yet capable of sustaining thought-images and emotions: something, in short, which is a bridge between matter and mind. This psychic aether, I postulate, is organized into specific form in the presence of ordinary matter: to put it crudely, there is an aetheric duplicate of every material object. It is this duplicate, I believe, which the mind apprehends . . . in clairvoyance and which it controls . . . in psychokinesis. . . . An aetheric world of this sort, with its own phenomena and laws, seems to me something we may be driven to recognize. Professor H. H. Price postulates it to account for hauntings and apparitions . . . I believe it is also involved in poltergeist phenomena and is of special interest and great importance in the structure of Man himself. We shall therefore introduce the idea here. It may, of course, ultimately go the way of the physicist's aether as knowledge develops, but it probably takes us just a step nearer to the ultimately real from the ordinary matter of physics and chemists."

If this does exist, it is not difficult to understand the astral body. In fact, Johnson says, "From such a viewpoint we should expect man himself to have an aetheric body or vehicle, for the organized psychic aether would be the mold or prototype of his physical body."

According to this concept, then, psychic ether is the substance which interconnects or intermingles with the physical and the spiritual planes of existence. Because it is imperceptible to our physical senses it is ignored by us on earth except, as now, when we are trying to explain psychic phenomena. And apparently some phenomena can only be explained by admitting psychic ether's existence.

As witness that thought impression occurs, we have a spirit communication as our authority. If quoting such a source appears odd, I can only say that since we are dealing with such an other-worldly topic, for which we have no adequate interpretations of our own, we'd better take whatever help is available to us as long as it seems to be backed up by evidence. This message, received by automatic writing at the home of

Lord and Lady Radnor in England on February 27, 1890, is contributed by F. W. H. Myers in *Human Personality and Its Survival of Bodily Death.*

The automatic writing went: "You ask me whom I see in this habitation. I see many shades and several spirits. I see also a good many reflections. Can you tell me if a child died upstairs? Was there an infant who died rather suddenly? Because I continually see the shadow of an infant upstairs, near to the room where you dress. Yes, it is only a shadow."

Now, it was true that an infant brother of Lord Radnor's had died in convulsions in a nursery which then occupied the part of the house to which the communication referred. And Lord Radnor was sure that the automatist (the lady who was receiving the automatic writing) could not have known either of the death of his infant brother nor of the fact of that part of the house having previously been a nursery. But he did not know what this communicator meant by a "shadow." He asked, and the writing replied that a shadow is "when anyone thinks so continuously of a person that he imprints the shadow or memory on the surrounding atmosphere." In fact, he constructs a thought form. Would it be of the psychic ether that this form is made?

This idea is helpful in explaining hauntings, as well. The Radnor communicator said, "I myself am inclined to think that so-called ghosts of those who have been murdered . . . are more often shadows than earthbound spirits; for the reason that they are ever in the thoughts of the murderer, and so he creates, as it were, their shadow or image."

Now, this is not to imply that there may not be actual ghosts who are the spirits of deceased persons attempting to bring a message or to make their presence known for some possible reasons, either helpful or nefarious, of their own. There may be and there may not be; but that is not now the subject of our inquiry. What we are talking about here are *hauntings*, those vague apparitions which occasionally appear in a certain locality, apparently aimlessly recreating some familiar scene, or some anguishing event. They may very well have been formed by the powerful thoughts which occurred at that crucial moment. Myers has given the term "veridical after-image" to this phenomenon.

In *Nurslings of Immortality* Raynor Johnson adds to this: "I think it is plausible that the psychic aether in some places has been saturated by some strong emotional imagery, and there is in effect a kind of reservoir of energy at the place which cannot be dissipated except when it is visited by a person of the right telepathic affinity. One person in such a place may feel a vague unrest or aversion to it, another of the right quality may see a full-blown apparition. . . ."

I can see no reason to suppose that a veridical after-image impressed on the psychic ether might not include a much larger image than that of one puny ghost; and this is exactly what I suspect has happened in certain instances. It is reported that some battles of bygone wars are repeated on occasion, primarily from the point of view of sound. Persons who live near a large battleground of the War of Roses insist that at given times all the noises of the battle can be heard again. The booms of the cannons, the screams of the injured, the moans of the dying, and the shouts and all other uproar apparently still exist somewhere in some form; and, under certain as yet unknown conditions, can be heard by those "with the right telepathic affinity."

On August 4, 1951, two women, who are referred to by pseudonyms, Mrs. Dorothy Norton, age 32, and her sister-in-law, Miss Agnes Norton, 33, were on a holiday near Dieppe, France. There they had a collective auditory hallucination to end all collective auditory hallucinations, for they were awakened by all the sounds of British commando air raids. Starting at 4:20 a.m. and continuing at intervals until after 6 o'clock they heard waves of sound, first like a storm at sea which ebbed and flowed, then cries, shouts, and gunfire. They heard rifle shots and dive bombers. And eventually they heard a lot of men singing. The time of the various waves of sound actually coincided with the hours when the British commandos had raided Dieppe in August, 1942.

The two women gave corroborating independent accounts to the Society for Psychical Research. And the case went down in the history of parapsychology as an instance of retrocognition—which only means that by some form of extrasensory perception the women supernormally apprehended sounds from an earlier time. But how or why they apprehended them is not made clear. If they were not mutually imagining the experience, how is it explained? Nobody really knows. Is it too much like a plot of television's "twilight zone" to suppose that scenes from wars have imprinted themselves on the psychic ether, to reappear to certain psychic individuals afterwards?

This trend of thought leads us inevitably to Misses Jourdain and Moberly, whose story has been told so frequently that it is hardly necessary to give it much time here. In the gardens of Versailles these two prim, precise, and proper English ladies, daughters of Church of England clergymen, despisers of anything smacking of "occultism," had an experience that upset their prim, precise, and proper lives forevermore. Miss Anne Moberly, teacher in a girls' school in Oxford, England, and her friend Miss Eleanor Jourdain, lecturer in French at Oxford University, made a visit to Versailles on August 10, 1901. In the Petit Trianon they suddenly found themselves transported into another age—the actual period of Marie Antoinette.

They then witnessed and even took a speaking part in a scene from the life of the tragic queen as it had probably been enacted just before her imprisonment in 1799. Even the scenery they saw there was different from the way it actually existed in 1901; and the workmen, attendants, footmen, and all the women there were dressed in costumes of the earlier period. An air of inexplicable depression permeated all. The two ladies walked through the garden and came out the other side comparing notes as to what they had actually seen. Both had witnessed the same thing, although their intellects told them it could not have been real.

They spent years afterwards trying to check every detail. They inquired if there might have been a play rehearsal or a fete or anything which could account for the costumes and activities they saw; but nothing of that nature had been going on there. Nothing but an impression on the psychic ether which they happened to be sensitive enough to observe and participate in?

Several books have been published attempting to debunk this story, attacking the personal credibility and character of the women as well as their powers of observation. But to back them up there is Professor Charles Richet's statement that many citizens of Paris have come to him, knowing him to be the leader of French psychical research, to tell him of similar experiences of their own at Versailles.

In *How To Make ESP Work For You* Harold Sherman, the writer who had such conclusive telepathic communication with Sir Hubert Wilkins when he was on a trip to the North Pole, tells of a similar case. It was reported to him by a Miss Liebs, one of the first female symphony orchestra conductors in this country. She had been put into a little-used room in a crowded Atlantic City hotel and had there seen re-enacted a murder which had been committed the year before. She was told that she was the third occupant of that room who had witnessed this apparitional performance.

Sherman says, "It was years later that Miss Liebs gave me this account of her shocking experience, but she still was emotionally aroused by recollection of it. She asked me how I could explain it. I told her frankly that I didn't know; that there had been many similar experiences, too many to be ascribed to self-delusion or hallucination or fearsome imagination. Moreover, those seeing the apparitions had had no prior knowledge of the crime or tragic happening.

"I conjectured that, in some way we couldn't understand as yet, an energetic force field had been set up which had the power to reproduce this highly emotionalized event. It was almost as though the thought forms cast off by the violent act were still existent in a kind of synthetic life and pattern of their own. Then, when people came into this atmosphere and went to sleep, thus blanking their conscious minds, their extrasensory faculties were activated by the vibrations surrounding them. Once tuned in, the force of these vibrations caused them to awaken and they remained fixated, almost mesmerized, until the extrasensory drama had run its course.

"It is once more worth observing that intense feeling was associated with this event. That a lingering condition can be set up in the atmosphere and physical properties of rooms and areas, is suggested by the fact that, when rooms or buildings or other locales have been torn down, greatly altered, or cleaned up and renovated, ESP phenomena have disappeared. Whatever force has been existent there, set in motion by the original happening, apparently has been dissipated, destroyed or at least released."

Whether or not we believe the reasons put forth here by way of explanation, we are just about forced from the evidence to acknowledge that such incidents do occur. In view of such evidence, which can only be ignored by closing one's mind to it, I am submitting a proposition: If doubles of living persons can appear to themselves and to others; if images of the deceased can haunt; if vardøger or the sounds of living people can precede them; and if visions of past events can reappear as if in actuality—there must be a condition that causes it. That isn't too startling a proposition, is it? To me it is not too far-fetched to assume that this condition is the psychic ether, just awaiting the invention of some new mechanism, on the idea of a radio, which can make it evident to our physical senses.

But whether or not this is the answer, something has to be. As Ivan Sanderson says, "I'll go for coincidence up to three times, and after that I'll look for a law."

14

Close Calls and Permanent Projections

GEORGE C. RITCHIE OF RICHMOND, VIRGINIA, HAD JUST COMPLETED basic training at Camp Barkeley, Texas, early in December, 1943, and was getting ready to take a train to Richmond to enter medical school as part of the Army's doctor-training program. He says, "It was an unheard-of break for a private, and I wasn't going to let a chest cold cheat me out of it." But he was suffering from more than a chest cold, and the night he was to leave on the train for Richmond he became much worse. While being X-rayed, he fainted. Then, as he states in *Guideposts*, June, 1963: "When I opened my eyes, I was lying in a little room I had never seen before. . . . For a while I lay there, trying to recall where I was. All of a sudden I sat bolt upright. The train! Now I'd miss the train!"

"Now I know that what I am about to describe will sound incredible," Ritchie says. "I do not understand it any more than I ask you to; all that I can do is relate the events as they occurred." He sprang out of bed and looked around the room for his uniform. As he glanced back, he stopped, staring. Someone was lying in the bed he had just left.

"I stepped closer in the dim light, then drew back," he writes. "He was dead. The slack jaw, the gray skin were awful. Then I saw the ring. On his left hand was the Phi Gamma Delta fraternity ring I had worn for two years."

Ritchie ran into the hall, eager to escape the mystery of that room. Outside were people, but no one could see him. He was unable to make contact with anything he touched. He was confused, but as his mind became clearer, he says, "I was beginning to know too that the body on that bed was mine, unaccountably separated from me, and that my job was to get back and rejoin it as fast as I could."

He had difficulty finding his body when he returned to the hospital, and when he finally found it, a sheet had been drawn over the face. He recognized himself by the fraternity ring on the hand outside the blanket. He tried to draw back the sheet, but could not seize it, and then suddenly, "This is death," he thought. "This is what we human beings call death, this splitting up of one's self."

Then the room began to fill with light, with love. "That room was flooded, pierced, illuminated, by the most total compassion I have ever felt. It was a presence so comforting, so joyous and all-satisfying that I wanted to lose myself forever in the wonder of It." Simultaneously with this Christ presence something else was in that room—every single episode of his entire life, and each asked the question, "What did you do with your time on earth?"

Then Ritchie's consciousness expanded to take in wider vision. He writes: "I followed Christ through ordinary streets and countrysides . . . thronged with people. People with the unhappiest faces I ever had seen. Each grief seemed different. I saw businessmen walking the corridors of the places where they had worked, trying vainly to get someone to listen to them. I saw a mother following a sixty-year-old man, her son I guessed, cautioning him, instructing him. He did not seem to be listening.

"Suddenly I was remembering myself, that very night, caring about nothing but getting to Richmond. Was it the same for these people; had their hearts and minds been all concerned with earthly things, and now, having lost earth, were they still fixed hopelessly here? I wondered if this was hell. To care most when you are most powerless; this would be hell indeed."

He was permitted to look at two more worlds, but they were too real, too solid to be called "spirit worlds," he felt. He saw a realm where the absorption was not with worldly things but with truth—sculptors and philosophers, composers and inventors, great universities and libraries and scientific laboratories that surpass the wildest inventions of science fiction. Then he saw a great city of light—it was blinding in its beauty.

And then he woke up in his bed. Before he left the hospital cured he caught a glimpse of his chart. On it he read: "Pvt. George Ritchie, died December 20, 1943, double lobar pneumonia." He talked to his doctor later and was told the same thing, that he had been dead, but that a shot of adrenalin had brought him back to life. Ritchie says, "My return to life, he told me, without brain damage or other lasting effect, was the most baffling circumstance of his career."

Guideposts states that it has in its possession affidavits from both the Army doctor and attending nurse on the case which attest to the fact that Dr. Ritchie had been pronounced dead.

Apparently it is not rare for a person who is said to have died momentarily to have an out-of-body experience during that interim. And once in a while someone who dies permanently may somehow send a thought picture ahead to carry the message of his sorry plight to a loved one.

In Glasgow, Scotland, on April 4, 1913, Miss Mary M. Paterson had two visions of her brother Edgar, who was in Australia. As she walked out of a lecture hall she was startled to see reflected in the air in front of her a clear-cut picture of her brother in Australia. He was lying with the unmistakably helpless look of a dead or unconscious man who had just fallen. "I saw his pose, his clothes, and even his thick curling hair as if in life before me," she says. The picture faded, but later came back again as she was walking along the road.

The next week a cablegram came from Melbourne announcing the death on April 7th of her brother. Miss Paterson had seen him in her vision three days before his death as he had suddenly fallen down unconscious on the ship while travelling home from New Zealand to Melbourne.

Edgar obviously had an astral projection of some sort, but he was probably not aware of it; although how did his picture seek out his sister in Glasgow unless his consciousness, somewhere, willed it there?

Completely aware of what she was doing, and satisfied with the result was Mrs. William Birbeck, who had left her home in Seattle and travelled alone to Scotland. On her return trip she was taken ill at Cockermouth, England. Her husband and three children had remained in Seattle, where, one morning, the children sat up in their beds excitedly. "Mamma has been here," they cried, all having seen her and heard her speak to them.

That same morning in Cockermouth she had said, "I should be ready to go if I could but see my children once more." She then closed her eyes. After about ten minutes of stillness she reopened them, looked up brightly and said, "I have been with my children." Then peacefully she died. The two incidents coincided exactly in time when checked later, according to the account in the *Proceedings* of the Society for Psychical Research.

A man Eileen Garrett saw as an apparition both before and after his death is described in *Telepathy*. Teddy was a boy whom she had known and liked in her early youth in Ireland, but she had lost sight of him in the intervening years. One evening in London she had a vision of him and he told her his mother was dying. This she later learned was true.

Eileen and Teddy became good friends afterwards when he came to London to live, and then he went to India, from whence he wrote her cheerfully and often. She says: "One evening three years after his departure for India, I had a vivid impression of seeing Teddy standing close to me. He seemed to be ill, and he clearly made an effort to communicate something to me, but the strain was too much for him, and in a brief moment the vision faded away. . . . Disturbed by my failure to understand his message, I picked up a pencil in the hope that I might get some impressions from him automatically. Immediately I began to write: 'Dear long-haired pal, I feel the need to talk with you tonight. I have been very sick these few days—a touch of the sun, maybe. Lately I have been weary of living, and tonight I am strangely sad and alone. . . .' "

The writing stopped abruptly, and afterwards Eileen decided that the communication was probably a product of her subconscious mind. Later, however, she had a letter from a friend of Teddy's announcing his death, and enclosing a portion of a letter to her he had never finished. "Dear long-haired pal," it began, and continued with the exact lines she had received by automatic writing.

There are countless stories of apparitions seen at the instant of death, or just before—or just after. Sometimes it is not possible to distinguish the exact moment.

Mrs. Gaylord Hancock of Moravian Falls, North Carolina, writes me, "I have been interested in psychic phenomena ever since my English-born grandmother told me as a child about seeing the apparition of her mother come through her bed-curtains and smile at her when the mother actually lay dying in another room." Asked for amplification of this story, Mrs. Hancock says: "My grandmother's name was Harriet Wilkinson and until she was eighteen years old she lived in a small village named Methwold in Lincolnshire, England. I never knew her to tell a lie, and so I didn't question the story she told me about seeing her mother at the time of her death.

"She knew that her mother was very sick because all of the kinfolk were gathered about in her room. They put little Harriet to bed in another room. The bed was a high four-poster with a small ladder to climb up on. It had heavy curtains all around, and the curtains were drawn. Harriet didn't go to sleep. 'Suddenly,' she told me, 'I saw my mother pull apart the curtains on the side of the bed. She smiled at me and disappeared.' "

Harriet knew her mother was too sick to get out of bed—and yet she saw her standing beside her. It was soon after this that she learned that her mother had died.

Next we have a story told by a woman who while herself having an out-of-body experience, welcomed the spirit of a dying man into the nebulous and unknown world in which they both seemed to be existing at that moment.

Mrs. Mary Stuart Albrecht, nicknamed Maidie, is a very organized person who keeps her eye on the clock frequently throughout the day, and does many things by rote. She always listens to the 11 o'clock news on the radio each night, and retires at 11:15. Her very systematic nature makes her story more believable. How could anyone who keeps such careful account of herself and the time, give us a garbled report of her out-of-body experience? (Her daughter Nina confirms all the parts of the story within her personal knowledge.)

The other two members of our cast of characters are Mrs. Albrecht's husband Arthur, who died in 1945, and his lifelong friend Will Reichert. Will lived with his wife two blocks from Columbia Presbyterian Medical Center on W. 168th Street in New York City. The two men had been schoolmates, and since their marriages their families had continued the friendship. Will Reichert was a very slight, slim man with a boyish figure. He was completely bald.

One night in the early spring of 1948 Mrs. Albrecht turned off her radio and light at precisely 11:15 and slipped into bed. As soon as her eyes were closed she was standing on a corner of the street across from the building in which the Reicherts lived. (This did not seem like a dream to her, but absolute reality—yet it had the dreamlike quality of acceptance of what occurred without question.) On the opposite corner Mrs. Albrecht saw her husband Arthur, who had been dead three years. With joy she ran with outstretched arms to greet him. He didn't even look at her, for his gaze was fastened on the Reichert apartment house; but he reached out his hand and took his wife's in a warm grasp.

Then began a series of fifteen-minute intervals, Mrs. Albrecht waking up and looking at her clock, waiting five minutes and closing her eyes again and immediately being back with her husband. The fourth and final interval found them walking toward the hospital and entering a ward. Then Arthur left Maidie and told her not to follow. She peeked through the door of the room into which he had gone and found herself looking into a doctor's office. She could see the desk, with prescription blanks, and even a stethoscope upon it. What she couldn't understand was that there was a bed in the middle of this office. Just then her husband returned, leading by the hand a slight figure who looked like a young boy, his head covered with dark hair. Maidie ran to meet them, and realized she was seeing Will Reichert with the physical appearance of his youth; but his eyes were as expressionless as a zombie's. Her husband then took her hand, and walking three abreast they traversed the two blocks back to the Reichert home. When Will saw his own apartment house he became more alert; but Maidie doesn't know what he did, for it was time for her to be home again. Suddenly she came to herself, with the conviction that Will Reichert was dead. She told Nina so the next morning, and shortly thereafter it was confirmed by his wife on the telephone.

Mrs. Albrecht, in order to verify the things she had seen, asked judicious questions, and learned that Mr. Reichert had suffered a sudden heart attack the night before. There was not a single room available in the hospital, and so his doctor had given up his office space, and a bed had been placed in there for Will. He had died around twelve o'clock.

Now, in the past I would listen to a story like this and be very interested, but a tiny bit skeptical. Even after reading countless case histories and interviewing numberless people for their personal experiences, I was one of those who had to be shown. While not exactly from Missouri, and endeavoring to maintain an open mind, I still have always found it more easy to comprehend phenomena when I have had personal contact with them, or something similar. (Even when I have a psychic encounter of my own, I argue with it. "Maybe it was my subconscious mind"; "maybe it was poor observation"; "maybe it was colored by my own desires and wishes." You know. You probably do the same thing.)

But I must admit that the concept of out-of-body travel is more easy for me to accept since I personally had a small experience of my own. Early on the morning of September 3, 1963, in a London hotel I awoke and then lay quietly in a half-awake, half-asleep state. Suddenly I was in an unidentifiable place greeting a deceased friend. All the conditions were so totally different from a dream that while the warm hugging and kissing of long separated friends was going on I thought to myself, "But this is not a dream! This is real!" There and then I realized that I must be having an astral projection. I did go through a dream state to come out of the other state; but that was clearly recognizable as a dream and totally different from the actual reality of the previous one. The rest of that day I was more elated than I had ever been before in my life.

The passage of time has dimmed the immediacy of the episode; rationalization has said it must have been a particularly vivid dream; the fact that no evidence was procured has made it diminish in value. But the knowledge that numerous others have had similar experiences from which evidence *was* acquired has kept a little flame of excitement burning in me. *Was* it real out-of-body activity? Is it after all possible to see a loved friend who has passed into a spirit world of some description? Do such instances really have evidential value to prove the survival of the human spirit? Or do I, and all the rest, have an hallucination syndrome? Frankly, I must admit that the testimony of others is definitely more conclusive if you have also been there.

The great Dr. Carl Jung went through the same arguments when he had a personal adventure which was much more valuable than mine. Here is his account quoted from *Memories, Dreams, Reflections:*

"One night I lay awake thinking of the sudden death of a friend whose funeral had taken place the day before. I was deeply concerned. Suddenly I felt that he was in the room. It seemed to me that he stood at the foot of my bed and was asking me to go with him. I did not have the feeling of an apparition; rather, it was an inner visual image of him, which I had explained to myself as a fantasy. But in all honesty I had to ask myself, 'Do I have any proof that this is a fantasy? Suppose it is not a fantasy, suppose my friend is really here and I decided he was only a fantasy—would that not be abominable of me?' Yet I had equally little proof that he stood before me as an apparition. Then I said to myself, 'Proof is neither here nor there! Instead of explaining him away as a fantasy, I might just as well give him the benefit of the doubt and for experiment's sake credit him with reality.' The moment I had that thought, he went to the door and beckoned me to follow him. So I was going to have to play along with him. That was something I hadn't bargained for. I had to repeat my argument to myself once more. Only then did I follow him in my imagination.

"He led me out of the house, into the garden, out to the road, and finally to his house. (In reality it was several hundred yards away from mine.) I went in, and he conducted me into his study. He climbed on a stool and showed me the second of five books with red bindings which stood on the second shelf from the top. Then the vision broke off. I was not acquainted with his library and did not know what books he owned. Certainly I could never have made out from below the titles of the books he had pointed out to me on the second shelf from the top.

"This experience seemed to me so curious that next morning I went to his widow and asked whether I could look up something in my friend's library. Sure enough, there was a stool standing under the bookcase I had seen in my vision, and even before I came closer I could see the five books with red bindings. I stepped up on the stool so as to be able to read the titles. They were translations of the novels of Emile Zola. The title of the second volume read: *The Legacy of the Dead*. The contents seemed to me of no interest. Only the title was extremely significant in connection with this experience."

Certainly Jung did not believe himself to be having an actual projection; but he did think he went into the man's home, and he brought back evidence. Extrasensory perception acquired via a vision might be the answer.

Next we have a story of a man who really saw a ghost in broad daylight. He protests his objectivity, but not too much—just enough to be convincing. Lieut. James J. Larkin of the Royal Air Force gives his account of the events of December 7, 1918, to the *Journal* of the S.P.R. as follows:

He says that his friend, Lt. David E. M'Connell, in his flying clothes, came into his room at 11:30 and told him he was flying to Tadcaster drome, saying: "I expect to get back in time for tea. Cheerio."

Larkin says, "What I am about to say now is extraordinary to say the least, but happened so naturally that at the time I did not give it a second thought. I have heard and read of similar happenings and I must say that I always disbelieved them absolutely. My opinion had always been that the persons to whom these appearances were given were people of a nervous, highly-strung, imaginative temperament, but I had always been among the incredulous ones and had been only too ready to pooh-pooh the idea. I was certainly awake at the time, reading and smoking."

After lunch Larkin had spent the afternoon writing letters and reading. He was sitting in front of the fire shortly before

3:30, the door of the room being about eight feet away at his back. He heard someone walking up the passage; the door opened with the usual noise and clatter which David always made, and Larkin heard his "Hello, boy!" He turned half around in his chair and saw David standing in the doorway, half in and half out of the room, holding the door knob in his hand. He was dressed in his full flying clothes and there was nothing unusual in his appearance. Larkin says, "His cap was pushed back on his head and he was smiling, as he always was when he came into the rooms and greeted us. In reply to his 'Hello, boy!' I remarked, 'Hello! back already?' He replied, 'Yes, got there all right, had a good trip.' Then he concluded, 'Well, cheerio!' closed the door noisily and went out." Larkin was looking at him the whole time he was speaking.

When he learned later in the evening that M'Connell had crashed, Larkin could not believe it was on the Tadcaster journey, for he knew he had seen him after he arrived home from that. However, the facts were that he had been killed while flying to Tadcaster, presumably at 3:25, since that was the time his watch had stopped.

Larkin says, "I tried to persuade myself that I had not seen him or spoken to him in this room, but I could not make myself believe otherwise, as I was undeniably awake and his appearance, voice, manner had all been so natural. I am of such a skeptical nature regarding things of this kind that even now I wish to think otherwise, that I did not see him, but I am unable to do so."

I won't give many more ghost stories, because I don't want to scare anyone. A few which bring evidence should suffice. The first is a woman seen for the first time as an apparition who presents such well-defined features that her son can later be recognized by the resemblance.

Mrs. Margot Moser of Jamaica, Long Island, a nurse, writes me: "In the winter of 1948-49 I nursed a very sick old lady, Mrs. Rosa B. She was a very clever, well-educated, and highly cultured immigrant from Odessa, Russia, who had lived for many years in New York City. She was residing at that time at the Savoy Plaza Hotel on Fifth Avenue, and up to the last she was mentally competent.

"Early one afternoon I had put my patient to bed for a nap and was sitting at my little table beside the window writing in her chart. I was facing her bed, the door at my back. Mrs. B. had been asleep, but suddenly I saw her sit up and wave happily, her face all smiles. I turned my head toward the door, thinking one of her daughters had come in; but much to my surprise it was an elderly lady I had never seen before. She had a striking resemblance to my patient— the same light blue eyes, but a longer nose and heavier chin. I could see her very clearly for it was bright daylight; the window shades were only slightly lowered. The visitor walked toward my patient, bent down, and, as far as I can remember, they kissed each other. But then, as I got up and walked toward the bed, she was gone.

"Mrs. B. looked very pleased. She took my hand and said, 'It is my sister!' Then she slept peacefully again. I saw the same apparition twice later on, but never as clearly and always from another room. But every time she came the patient was obviously elated.

"At Mrs. B.'s funeral service some weeks later, I positively identified a gentleman as being the son of the apparition, because he had his mother's nose and chin and looked so much like her. I asked one of the daughters about it, and she said that he *was* her cousin."

Our next apparition doesn't do anything but show herself, but she manages to do so in a bonnet which is so unusual that it brings evidence to her grandson. Who was the grandson? None other than our Reverend Tweedale, he whose vardøger preceded him home. On the night of his grandmother's death and before they had heard the news of it, both he and his father saw her apparition; and it was wearing the old-fashioned frilled or goffered cap which she wore at the time of her death. Such a cap her grandson had never seen on her in life.

This enterprising ghost also showed herself to her daughter and even spoke to her. But her main goal in making her post-mortem appearance seemed only to tell members of the family of her death.

I now give an account of an apparition who came with an important purpose and had no time for idle chitchat.

Miss Lucy Dodson, an English lady, writes: "On June 5, 1887, a Sunday evening, between eleven and twelve at night, I was in bed, but not asleep. The room was lighted by a gaslight in the street outside. I heard my name called three times. I answered twice, thinking it was my uncle, 'Come in, Uncle George, I am awake'; but the third time I recognized the voice as that of my mother, who had been dead sixteen years. I said, 'Mamma!'

"She then came round a screen near my bedside with two sleeping children in her arms, and placed them in my arms and put the bedclothes over them and said, 'Lucy, promise me to take care of them, for their mother is just dead.' I said, 'Yes, Mamma.' She repeated, 'Promise me to take care of them.' I replied, 'Yes, I promise you'; and I added, 'Oh, Mamma, stay and speak to me, I am so wretched.' [I was out of health, and in anxiety about family troubles.] She replied, 'Not yet, my child,' and then she went round the screen again; and I remained, feeling the children to be still in my arms, and fell asleep. When I awoke there was nothing."

Now the background of this story is as follows: The forty-two-year-old Miss Dodson had a younger brother whom she helped to raise after her mother's death. He had married two years before, and she had not seen him since, although she had heard of the birth of a little girl in January of the previous year. She had never seen his wife, and did not know that she was again pregnant.

Miss Dodson told her uncle the next morning about the apparition she had seen, but, she says, "He thought I was sickening of brain fever." However, they soon were to learn that on June 5th about nine o'clock at night her sister-in-law had died, shortly after the birth of a son. "It was between eleven and twelve o'clock the same night that my mother brought me the two little children," Miss Dodson writes. Their ages corresponded to those of her sister-in-law's babies— a little girl perhaps a year-and-a-half old and a newborn boy.

This case meets enough of the criteria for veridicality to enable us safely to say that it was more than a mere hallucination on the part of Miss Dodson, since by it she gained information she had not previously had; it gave evidence of continued interest in earth affairs by a spirit; and the apparition conversed with her. Its main defect is that it is an old case which depends upon the testimony of the percipient; and that we have in some way to account for the apparitions of the living children. Were they having out-of-body experiences, at their age! Or were they thought forms created by the spirit who brought them? This is really a complicated one, isn't it?

A more modern ghost who conveys information and does not present all these other problems visited Chester Hayworth (another pseudonym for a man whose real name is on file with the American Society for Psychical Research) in Dallas, Texas, in 1949.

After teaching a class in astronomy at the Y.M.C.A., Hayworth returned home about midnight and climbed into bed quietly without disturbing his wife. Just then his father, who lived in California, walked through the bedroom door. Hayworth thought he had flown in as a surprise. He says: "I watched him as he walked across the room, around the foot of the bed, up to and opposite me. He stopped and stood two feet or less from where I was sitting. I was waiting for him to speak to me. By now I had a good look at his face, and I knew he was not here to carry out some joke on me. I had never seen my father looking so sad, downcast or forlorn. I knew at once that something was wrong. I thought perhaps some dreadful thing had happened to a member of the family and he was here to prepare me for the worst."

Apparently from shock and surprise, Hayworth was speechless. His father extended his hand.

"I took it in mine," Hayworth wrote. "He squeezed my hand and held it, much harder than his usual handshake."

Even though they didn't speak, the father seemed to read the son's thoughts as he wondered if something tragic had happened to his mother or brother.

"Still holding my hand in his," says Hayworth, "he moved his head from side to side in a negative way, and then suddenly he disappeared, leaving me with my outstretched hand in mid-air, gazing at nothing."

But while this inconceivable interlude was going on, Hayworth had a good enough look at his father to see that he was dressed in tan work pants, a tan shirt and cap—the kind of outfit he wore only rarely, when working on his car. He had on brown suspenders, and in his shirt pocket his son noted three objects—a pencil, a fountain pen, and a caliper rule.

Hayworth was soon to learn that his father had died a short time before his midnight social call, having passed away suddenly while tinkering with his car. Hayworth went to California for the funeral, and while there he looked at the clothing his father had worn at the time of his death. The costume was identical with what the apparition wore, even to the caliper rule in the shirt pocket.

Sometimes a ghost doesn't have to talk in order to impart information.

15

The

Faintly-Glowing Mist

ANDREW JACKSON DAVIS WAS AN AMERICAN MEDIUM OF THE last century who endeavored in his extremely obscure books to explain life, death, and the hereafter as he had learned about them through his clairvoyant abilities. In *Great Harmonia* he described a scene he had witnessed at the death of an individual unknown to him. He saw the spiritual body withdraw itself from the mortal and issue from the head of the dying person, first as a cloud of luminosity which hovered above the bed and was attached by a fine luminous cord to the head. This cloud then slowly took the form of the person, a bright shining image a little smaller than the physical body but a perfect replica. This hovered over the recumbent mortal body, attached to it by the cord of light just as a captive balloon might be moored to the ground.

Now this might somehow tie in with what we have been told about astral bodies, and it might also give indication that all haunts are not mere veridical after-images. This something which some persons claim to see leave the physical body at death might be at least a basic constituent of ghostliness, material of which a future apparition is constructed.

Others have seen it, too. Our ubiquitous Mr. Tweedale is among the first to present us with a case. He writes that such a hovering spirit was observed at the passing of his wife's mother, Mary Burnett, which occurred on July 29, 1921, at

Sunderland. During the night Tweedale's wife, his daughter Marjorie, and the nurse, were watching by the bedside of the unconscious Mrs. Burnett. The room was brightly lighted, when, just past midnight, "Suddenly Marjorie saw a small cloud of grey smoke, which she describes as something like the smoke from a cigarette, hovering over the form of Mrs. Burnett as she lay in bed. At first it appeared to be about three or four inches in diameter, and it floated in the air a few inches above the bedclothes and directly over the abdomen of the unconscious woman."

All three watched as it gradually grew in size until it became as large as a dinner plate. The upper part turned to a rich purple which hovered steadily a few inches above the recumbent form. Soon to their further astonishment a beautiful halo began to form around the head. During the hour in which these phenomena were visible, "My wife several times passed her hand through the hovering cloud of purple light without displacing it or meeting any resistance, but on closing her eyes the cloud and halo ceased to be visible, showing that they were objective and external to her eye."

Miss Dorothy Monk writes in *Light* the following account of what took place at her mother's deathbed on January 2, 1922:

". . . At dusk that afternoon as she lay perfectly quiet, my three sisters and I all at once noticed a pale blue-mauve haze all over her as she lay. We watched it and very gradually it deepened in color until it became a deep purple, so thick that it almost blotted out her features from view, and spread all in the folds of the bedclothes like a purple fog. . . . We thought it very wonderful, so called the two remaining sisters to see if they could see it too, and they could."

As they watched, very gradually patches of yellow, like sunlight, appeared on the pillow; one at the left side of her head was particularly bright sometimes, and then would slowly dim and once more become bright again. Miss Monk goes on: "Mother's old friend was also in the room during this time, but she neither saw the purple mist around mother nor the blue lights, and said that our eyes were tired with watching, and that we were overwrought. We drew her attention to this very bright patch on the pillow, and she saw it, but said it was the reflection of the fire or gaslight. We screened both, and then she went round the room and moved pictures and photograph frames and tilted the mirror, but without making any difference to the light. At last she came and put her hands directly over it, but without shading it in any degree; after that she sat down without saying a word."

When the American writer Louisa May Alcott and her mother and the family doctor were gathered at the deathbed of Miss Alcott's sister, they all witnessed something similar to that just described. The body of the patient shook with the tremor of death, the doctor made a final examination and prepared to pull the sheet over the corpse. Just then a thin, faintly glowing mist rose slowly from the body, coalesced, and floated away. Miss Alcott pictures the scene: "My mother's eyes followed mine and when I said, 'What did you see?' she described the same mist." The doctor also said that he had seen the faintly luminous mist; but he had no professional opinion to propound as to its nature.

That busy propounder of opinions Dr. Samuel Johnson once said, "There is no people, rude or unlearned, among whom apparitions of the dead are not related and believed. This opinion, which prevails as far as human nature is diffused, could only become universal by its truth. Those that never heard of one another could not have agreed upon a tale which nothing but experience could make credible."

Which brings us to an incident told by a missionary from Polynesia. In Tahiti, he said, "Prophets were supposed to speak under the influence of departed spirits, and these were thought still to retain the human form. At death the soul was believed to be drawn out of the head, whence it was borne away to be slowly and gradually united to the god from whom it had emanated. . . . Among the privileged few who have the blessed gift of clairvoyance, some affirm that, shortly after a human body ceases to breathe, a vapor arises from the head, hovering a little way above it but attached by a vapory cord. The substance, it is said, gradually increases in bulk and assumes the form of the inert body. When this has become quite cold, the connecting cord disappears and the disentangled soul-form floats away as if borne by invisible carriers."

Commenting on this excerpt from the *Metapsychical Magazine*, Ernesto Bozzano says: "Here we have a description which corresponds in the minutest particulars with those narrated by present-day clairvoyants. Having stated this, it does not seem logical or reasonable to attempt to explain such a startling agreement by recurring to the hypothesis of 'coincidence.' On the other hand, since the Tahitians cannot have drawn their beliefs from civilized peoples, and these cannot have drawn them from the Tahitians, it must perforce be recognized that from such comparisons there emerges a strong presumption in support of the objectivity of this phenomenon observed by clairvoyants of all times and among all peoples."

Now, if such appearances as these are reported on a worldwide basis, in primitive and civilized cultures, from the dawn of history to the present day—why, oh, why do not more scientists investigate and study and try to prove or disprove them? It is primarily a lack of information, I do believe. Since such things have been relegated to either folklore or religion, few scientists will give them attention, and so have never read the mounting mass of data which exists in support of them. But unfortunately, there will never be general acceptance or understanding of this subject until a great deal of time and effort are spent on it by trained investigators.

It certainly won't ever be possible to put an astral body or a veridical after-image into a test tube over a Bunsen burner; it may continue to be difficult to produce controlled experiments on demand; but continuous experimentation and observation will inevitably lead someone, someday, to an understanding of some of the immense potentialities of this fascinating subject.

Hereward Carrington has said, "If it could be shown photographically and instrumentally that something leaves the physical body at death, that would assuredly go a long way toward proving survival in some form—the persistence of some energy or entity separate and apart from the functional activities of the body."

There have been a few tests of this type, the most outstanding of which were performed by Dr. Duncan McDougall in 1906 when he was the head of the Massachusetts General Hospital. McDougall wished to determine whether there was any appreciable and detectable physical change which might be measurable in the human body when life ceased. He therefore had constructed a very delicate set of balance scales large enough to hold a bed and a dying patient. The scales were so delicate that they recorded even the added weight of a cigarette, when one was placed on the platform momentarily by an attendant.

Dr. McDougall and his associates weighed several patients during their terminal period and then at the instant of death. The first case was an elderly man with no known relatives. The scales at the exact moment of his death showed a sudden loss of weight of approximately one ounce. Taking into consideration the possible loss of air from the patient's lungs, there was still a measurable factor for which there was no ready accounting; so Dr. McDougall concluded that something real, although invisible, had left the patient's body as he died.

The experiment was repeated several times with other patients. Invariably the delicate scales indicated that something left the human body at death. Whatever it was, it weighed from a quarter of an ounce to slightly more than an ounce.

Now, in the last two chapters, we have given indication that apparitions of the living are seen before, and at the moment of death, and that apparitions of the dead look and behave in a manner similar to apparitions of the living. It is true that all apparitions cannot be presumed to be the actual vessels of the mind. Doppelgängers, vardøger, hauntings and other impressions on the psychic ether seem to have no conscious purpose. Yet, as we have seen, there are certain ghosts which do by their performance and even their conversation indicate that conscious intent and activity are present. We also have to consider the mist which is occasionally seen to escape at death, which parallels the astral body said to leave the physical organism of a living projectionist.

What does all this indicate as referred to our out-of-body discussion? Professor Ducasse warns us not to be too hasty in jumping at conclusions. In *The Belief in a Life After Death* he says:

"Persons who have had the out-of-the-body experience have usually assumed . . . that the spatial separation in it of the observing and thinking consciousness from the body on the bed means that the former is capable of existing and of functioning independently of the latter not only thus temporarily during projection, but enduringly at death, which is then simply permanent, definitive projection when the silver cord snaps.

"This conclusion, however, does not necessarily follow, for it tacitly assumes that the conscious double is what animates the body—normally in being collocated with it, but also, when dislocated from it, through connection with it by the silver cord. The fact, however, could equally be that the animation is in the converse direction, i.e., that death of the body entails death of the conscious double whether the latter be at the time dislocated from or collocated with the former.

"Hence, out-of-the-body experience, however impressive to those who have it, and however it may tempt them to conclude that they then know that consciousness is not dependent on the living material body, does not really warrant this conclusion; but only the more modest one, which, of course is arresting enough, that correct visual perception of physical events and objects, including perception of one's own body from a point distant in space from it, can occur, exceptionally, at times when the eyes are shut and the body asleep. . . ."

Hornell Hart, looking at the entire picture, which includes the activity of these deceased entities we've just been discussing, sees an altogether different prospect. "The phenomena of ESP projection," he says in "Six Theories About Apparitions," "show that at least a considerable proportion of apparitions of the living are vehicles of consciousness, and that the behavior of such apparitions is closely related to memory, purpose, emotional attachment, feelings of guilt, and other aspects of conscious personality. Suppose then that we array all evidential cases of apparitions in a distribution according to the length of time they occur before or after death. Assuming that consciousness is crucially dependent on the living physical brain, a sharp alteration should be evident in the character and behavior of apparitions when the death point in the array is passed. But *no such alteration is evident in the data.* . . ."

In view of this fact, and of the data previously presented, Dr. Hart submits "that the burden of proof now rests with those who would argue that apparitions provide no evidence of survival."

16

The Greatest Case
of All

PROFESSOR DUCASSE, RISING TO OUR CHALLENGE, TURNS OUT TO agree with us after all. He tells me that there is *one* case which he thinks is almost foolproof as survival evidence—the Watseka Wonder.

"But," I complained, "that won't fit into a book discussing the out-of-body enigma."

On second thought, he and I have decided that it might be the greatest out-of-body experience of all. The Watseka Wonder was thirteen-year-old Lurancy Vennum, whose conscious mind disappeared for three months while her body was ostensibly controlled by the spirit of another girl. If Lurancy wasn't out of her body, who ever was?

This is one of the best known and most thoroughly investigated cases in all psychical research. Not only was an account of it written and published at the time by Dr. E. Winchester Stevens, but Dr. Richard Hodgson of the Society for Psychical Research personally interviewed the members of both families and their friends about twelve years later. Dr. Hodgson's is hardly on-the-spot reporting, but the events had been so startling that they were still fresh even then in the minds of those involved. Objective as he attempted to be, and careful as he was not to commit himself to any rash statements, after his investigation Dr. Hodgson felt impelled to suggest that there seemed a strong likelihood that the highly controversial occurrences he was recording had actually taken place as told to him.

After all that buildup, the story goes like this: In Watseka, Illinois, in 1878, Mary Lurancy Vennum began to have what were thought to be fits. During them she would go into a trance and begin to talk like various other, usually disreputable, people. Finally, Dr. Stevens, a medical man who was also a spiritualist, was called in to investigate her condition. He suggested to her when she was in the trance state that some strong spirit entity should control her and keep the menacing intruders away. Lurancy then mentioned the name of Mary Roff as a spirit willing to help her. Mary had been a local girl who had died at the age of eighteen, when Lurancy was about fifteen months old.

The transfer of ownership of the body was accomplished the next day. Lurancy's consciousness completely disappeared during what was probably the longest abdication of a mind from a body on record. In its stead came the thinking apparatus, personality, and memories of Mary Roff. For the next three months this child who looked like thirteen-year-old Lurancy Vennum spoke and acted and thought and remembered like the eighteen-year-old Mary Roff who had died twelve years before.

Obviously uncomfortable in the Vennum home after the change had been effected, the girl was allowed to go and live with Mary Roff's parents. There she seemed to know everything and every person Mary had known in the past. She recognized and called by name those who were friends of her family. She remembered scores, yes, hundreds of incidents that had transpired during Mary's life.

To select an example from the numerous ones Dr. Stevens has reported, one evening while the child was out in the yard, Mr. Roff suggested as a test that his wife find a certain velvet headdress that Mary had worn the last year before she died.

He told her to lay it out and say nothing about it, to see if it would be recognized. Mrs. Roff readily found it and placed it on a stand. When Lurancy-Mary came in, she immediately exclaimed as she approached the stand, "Oh, there is my head-dress I wore when my hair was short!" She then asked, "Ma, where is my box of letters? Have you got them yet?" Mrs. Roff dug out a box stored in the attic. Examining it, the girl said, "Oh, Ma, here is a collar I tatted. Why didn't you show me my letters and things before?"

When Dr. Hodgson visited Mrs. Minerva Alter, Mary's sister, she told him many curious incidents. She assured him that the mannerisms and behavior of the child during the three months she was under the control of Mary Roff had strikingly resembled Mary Roff. The real Lurancy had barely met Mrs. Alter, but as Mary she embraced her affectionately and called her "Nervie." This was Mary's pet name for her sister, by which Mrs. Alter had not been called since Mary's death.

Lurancy-Mary stayed at Mrs. Alter's home for a while, and almost every hour of the day some trifling incident of Mary's life was recalled by her. One morning she said, "Right over there by the currant bushes is where Allie greased the chicken's eye." This incident had happened several years before Mary's death. Mrs. Alter remembered very well their cousin Allie treating the sick chicken's eye with oil. Allie now lived in Peoria, Illinois, and Lurancy had never known her.

One morning Mrs. Alter asked the girl if she remembered a certain old dog they had owned. Lurancy replied, "Yes, he died over there," pointing to the exact spot where the pet had breathed his last. Such things are not inordinately elegant as conversation goes, but as evidence of identity and personal memory, they are highly significant. The Roff family considered the many little things of this nature to be incontrovertible evidence that Mary was actually visiting them in this other body, no matter how strange the situation may have been.

When the term of Mary's tenure was up, it was declared that Lurancy was entirely healed and could return to her own body. This Lurancy did, and she was well from then on. The Roffs and Vennums had become friends—this experience of joint-ownership of a daughter had, not surprisingly, brought them close together. For some years afterwards, until Lurancy married and left home, whenever the parents visited together Lurancy would temporarily leave and Mary would control her body and chat with her father and mother.

Our Devil's Advocate questions the value of this case. He will point out the fact that the first account was written by a spiritualist, who believed in what he was saying and so could not be properly objective. He will note that the Hodgson investigation occurred twelve years later, when the memories of actual facts must have been dimmed by time and colored by constant repeating and checking against the memories of others. He may even suggest that Lurancy was a split—or alternating—personality, such as we have in recent years been familiar with in *The Three Faces of Eve,* the book by Thigpen and Cleckley and the award-winning movie.

Professor Ducasse says, however, that "what distinguishes this case from the more common ones of alternating personalities is, of course, that the personality that displaced Lurancy's was, by every test that could be applied, not a dissociated part of her own, but the personality and all the memories that had belonged to a particular eighteen-year-old girl who had died at the time when Lurancy was but fourteen months old." Dr. Ducasse points out that in no way consistent with the records could Lurancy have obtained by normal means the extensive and detailed knowledge of Mary's life, for the Vennums had lived away from Watseka the first seven years of Lurancy's life and then had barely known the Roff family.

Professor Ducasse concludes that "the only way that suggests itself, to avoid the conclusion that the Mary Roff personality which for fourteen weeks 'possessed' Lurancy's organism was really the departed spirit whom it pretended to be, is to have recourse to the method of orthodoxy, whose maxim is: 'When you cannot explain all the facts according to accepted principles, then explain those you can and ignore the rest; or else deny them, distort them, or invent some that would help.'"

He adds, . . . "Some facts turn out to be too stubborn to be disposed of plausibly by that method; and the present one would appear to be one of them."

17

Finale

THIS BOOK IS A COMPILATION OF DATA AND A DISCUSSION OF theories and ideas about a subject which does not fit within the framework of physical science as we know it today. What we have been dealing with are first steps that lead *up* to the gateway of science.

Even some parapsychologists do not classify out-of-body experiences as rating in importance with extrasensory perception and psychokinesis—which have been subjected to laboratory procedures and have come out with flying colors. Our topic is not so easy to test; and some of our best stories are not in the least documentable. Our main problem is, of course, that we have here to do with individuals and their testimony rather than with any reproducible and measurable phenomena. The word of a person who has undergone an exciting adventure is notoriously liable to error. And, anyway, witnesses whose attestations are perfectly acceptable in a court of law when they are speaking of an event as commonplace as an automobile accident, are seldom taken seriously about something so problematic and outside present knowledge as astral flying.

Yet the testimony of the kind of people, and the quantity of people, we have been quoting can hardly be thrown aside. "Doubt is justified only where it is a question of a deliberate lie," Aniela Jaffé affirms, adding that the number of cases of pure fabrication is small because "the authors of such fabrications are too ignorant to be able to lie properly."

Yram adds to this, "To suppose that I have been able to imagine all the details of the experiences I have related would be to endow me with qualities far more perfect than those needed in order to project the astral body. . . .

"In order to appreciate this properly you must remember that I am not telling you a dream, nor a vision. I am telling you of a real fact, a conscious act accomplished with an absolutely clear mind, with perfect freedom, and without any trace of sleep."

Yram states categorically, "There is no doubt concerning the part of self-projection. It is manifest to the most skeptical."

Yet even though Dr. Gardner Murphy, who is president of the American Society for Psychical Research, does not doubt the evidence presented by those who have experienced self-projection, he does not think of it as supernormal. For this reason he did not include out-of-body experiences in his book *Challenge of Psychical Research*. Listing them along with trance, ecstasy, depersonalization, and loss of individuality, he says, "All of these phenomena appear to be real . . ." but they are "not very far from the known terrain of general psychology, which we are beginning to understand more and more without recourse to the paranormal." Therefore, he says, there is no reason that can be offered for believing that they should be in a separate category of the psychical, rather than belonging to general psychology. And, Dr. Murphy adds, "There are dozens of published claims, often very dogmatic ones, about the aura, but I have not seen a serious experimental report on it."

It's the promotion of serious experimental reports that this book hopes to encourage. As another parapsychologist of perception, Margaret Eastman, of Oxford, says: "Few people would deny that out-of-the-body experiences are surprising. But it is not so widely realized that their surprisingness is important. They surprise us because they appear to contradict our conscious or unconscious assumption that at any rate in life we are indissolubly linked to our bodies and they to us—and this has an obvious bearing on our view of the universe. So to explain these experiences away merely by invoking vivid dreaming or hallucination is not good enough. The explanation may be true, but it is intellectually lazy to refuse to consider other possibilities—and intellectually inert to do nothing to establish it one way or another."

A case like the following, presented by a couple who are aware of the need for evidence and who have endeavored to procure it, cannot be ignored, and it deserves study and a "serious experimental report" if anything in the world ever did:

Mr. Lucien Landau writes in the *Journal* of the Society for Psychical Research, September, 1963: "I knew my wife, Eileen, for quite a number of years before we were married, and she frequently used to talk to me about her out-of-the-body experiences. These were of the usual kind, and on some occasions I was able to verify that something paranormal had, in fact, occurred."

One such incident happened when Landau was ill and Eileen was visiting at his home, occupying the spare bedroom which was opposite his room. "One morning," he says, "she told me that she came into my bedroom during the night (minus her physical body) to check my pulse and respiration. I asked her to do this again the following night, this time trying to bring some object with her; I gave her my small diary, weighing thirty-eight grams.

"That night we left the doors of both bedrooms open, as I could hardly expect a physical object to pass through solid wood. Before falling asleep, I asked myself to awake, should anything unusual occur in my room . . . [later] I woke up suddenly; it was dawn, and there was just about enough light coming in through the partly drawn curtains to enable one to read."

He saw in his room the figure of Eileen, looking straight ahead toward the window. She was wearing a nightdress, her face was extremely pale, almost white. The figure moved slowly backwards toward the door, but it was otherwise quite motionless; it was not actually walking. When it got out in the hall Landau rose from bed and followed. He says, "I could then clearly see the moving figure, which was quite opaque and looking like a living person, but for the extreme pallor of the face, and at the same time the head of Eileen, asleep in her bed, the bedclothes rising and falling as she breathed. I followed the figure, which moved all the time backwards looking straight ahead, but apparently not seeing me."

He stopped at the door of the spare bedroom, as the figure, now having reached a position beside the bed, suddenly vanished. There was no visible effect on Eileen, who did not stir, and whose rhythm of breathing remained unchanged.

Landau went back into his own room, and there, on the floor near the foot of his bed, he found a rubber toy dog which belonged to Eileen. It had previously been sitting on a small chest of drawers in her room.

Mrs. Landau's own report of the incident is appended to her husband's: "I remember getting out of bed (but do not recall exactly how), going over to my desk and seeing the diary. As a child, I had been told never to handle other people's letters or diaries, so probably for this reason I did not want to touch this one. Instead, I lifted my rubber toy dog, and I remember taking it through the door, across the landing, to the other room, but do not remember actually *walking*. I did not find the dog heavy, or difficult to hold. I have no recollection of what I finally did with it. I remember seeing Lucien asleep and breathing normally. I felt very tired and wanted to go back to bed. Up to this moment my consciousness appeared to me normal, and so did my ability to see my surroundings, which also appeared normal to me. I do not remember anything about going backwards to my room, or entering my bed." (Signed Eileen Landau.)

How can we doubt the truthful intent of such carefully observed and stated evidence? But how can we explain it?

And of what value is it? What would the understanding of such phenomena indicate concerning the nature of man?

That human being of great understanding, Dr. C. G. Jung says: "I have frequently seen people become neurotic when they content themselves with inadequate or wrong answers to the questions of life. They seek position, marriage, reputation, outward success or money, and remain unhappy and neurotic even when they have attained what they are seeking. Such people are usually confined within too narrow a spiritual horizon. Their life has not sufficient content, sufficient meaning. If they are enabled to develop into more spacious personalities, the neurosis generally disappears. . . . Among the so-called neurotics of our day are a good many who in other ages would not have been neurotic—that is, divided against themselves. If they had lived in a period and in a milieu in which man was still linked by myth with the world of the ancestors, and thus with nature truly experienced and not merely seen from outside, they would have been spared this division within themselves. I am speaking of those who cannot tolerate the loss of myth and who can neither find a way to a merely exterior world, to the world as seen by science, nor rest satisfied with an intellectual juggling with words, which has nothing whatsoever to do with wisdom."

There is a need for revolutionary changes in our philosophical way of thinking but we have not allowed ourselves to face it. This, as much as anything, is because of our fear of being considered unsophisticated if we let our thoughts dwell on something so old-fashioned as the concept of a "soul" and if we are simple enough to wonder what actually becomes of us after death. Yet when it is suggested by the material herein that it is possible for the human mind to leave the body on occasion while the body is alive, it is implied that the mind might also leave at the moment of death and survive when the physical body is destroyed. What this indicates is that survival of the consciousness is possible; and that is not an unhappy speculation for any of us in this ridiculous, frightening, seemingly purposeless world we live in.

F. W. H. Myers has said in his introduction to *Human Personality and Its Survival of Bodily Death* that to him the greatest paradox of human nature is the fact that man has never yet applied the methods of modern science to the problem which most profoundly concerns him—whether or not his personality involves any element which can survive bodily death.

Perhaps it is through the avenue of investigation of out-of-body experiences that this paradox can be solved. Professor W. H. C. Tenhaeff, Director of the Parapsychology Institute at the University of Utrecht in the Netherlands, believes so. He says, "It is of great importance that parapsychology research should . . . direct its attention to investigating so-called out-of-body experiences. If we have convincing facts regarding these experiences, we have made an important step forward on the road which can lead us in a scientifically justified manner to the belief in a personal survival after death."

After all, it was not too long ago that moon rockets and men orbiting the earth were pure science fiction. But when you begin dealing with the fringe of science, you sometimes end up with fringe benefits.

Bibliography

CHAPTER 1   TO INTRODUCE THE SUBJECT

Broad, C. D. *Lectures on Psychical Research,* The Humanities Press, New York, 1962.

Hales, Carol, "Astral Errand of Mercy," *Fate* Magazine, September, 1963, Vol. 16, No. 9.

Hart, Hornell "Man Outside His Body?" *Beyond the Five Senses,* J. B. Lippincott Co., New York, 1957.

Murchison, Carl (Ed.) *The Case For and Against Psychic Belief,* Clark University, Worcester, Mass., 1927.

Pratt, J. Gaither *Parapsychology,* Doubleday & Co., New York, 1964.

CHAPTER 2   SPONTANEOUS CASES

Aronowitz, Alfred C., and Hamill, Peter *Ernest Hemingway, The Life and Death of a Man,* Lancer Books, New York, 1961.

Crookall, Robert *The Study and Practice of Astral Projection,* The Aquarian Press, London, 1961.

Fate Magazine, November, 1963, Vol. 16, No. 11, February, 1964, Vol. 17, No. 2, p. 62.

Garrett, Eileen J. *Telepathy,* Creative Age Press, New York, 1945.

Guideposts, October, 1963.

Hemingway, Ernest, *A Farewell to Arms,* Charles Scribner's Sons, New York, 1929.

Journal of the American Society for Psychical Research, Vol. LVI, January, 1962, p. 28.

Jung, C. G. *Memories, Dreams, Reflections,* (Ed.) Aniela Jaffé, Pantheon Books, New York, 1961.

MacRobert, Russell G., "Where is Bridey Murphy?" *The Maple Leaf,* The Canadian Club of New York, Spring, 1956.

CHAPTER 3   HABITUAL TRAVELLERS

Fox, Oliver *Astral Projection,* University Books, New York, 1962.

Hankey, Muriel *J. Hewat McKenzie,* Helix Press, New York, 1963.

London Sunday Express, October 21, 1934.

Muldoon, Sylvan, and Carrington, Hereward *The Projection of the Astral Body*, Psychic Book Club, London, 1929.

—— *The Phenomena of Astral Projection*, Rider & Co., London, 1951.

—— *The Case for Astral Projection*, Aries Press, Chicago, 1936.

Whiteman, J. H. M. *The Mystical Life*, Faber & Faber, London, 1961.

Yram *Practical Astral Projection*, Samuel Weiser, New York (no date).

CHAPTER 4 THE ASTRAL BODY

Bendit, Phoebe Payne, and Laurence J. *The Psychic Sense*, E. P. Dutton & Co., Inc., New York, 1949.

Findlay, Arthur *The Way of Life*, Psychic Press, Ltd., London.

Garrett, Eileen J. *Adventures in the Supernormal*, Garrett Publications, New York, 1959.

Kilner, Walter J. *The Human Atmosphere*, Kegan Paul, London, 1920.

Kolb, Dr. Laurence C. *The Painful Phantom*, Charles C Thomas, Springfield, Ill., 1954.

Leadbeater, C. W. *Man Visible and Invisible*, The Theosophical Publishing House, India, 1952.

Schaffranke, Rolf "Secrets of the Human Aura," *Fate* Magazine, June, 1964, Vol. 17, No. 6.

Walther, Dr. Gerda "The Human Aura," *Tomorrow*, Spring, 1954. Vol. 2, No. 3.

White, Stewart Edward *The Betty Book*, E. P. Dutton & Co., New York, 1937.

Yogananda, Paramahansa *Autobiography of a Yogi*, Philosophical Library, New York, 1951.

CHAPTER 5 TO FIND THE MIND

Cummins, Geraldine *Beyond Human Personality*, Ivor Nicholson & Watson, Ltd., London, 1935.

Geley, Gustave *From the Unconscious to the Conscious*, Wm. Collins Sons & Co., Ltd., Glasgow, 1920.

Hart, Hornell *The Enigma of Survival*, Charles C Thomas, Springfield, Ill., 1959.

Johnson, Raynor C. *The Imprisoned Splendour*, Harper & Bros., New York, 1953.

Journal, American Medical Association, July 26, 1952.

MacRobert, Russell G. "Science Studies Intuition," *Tomorrow*, May, 1950, Vol. IX, No. 9.

Miller, R. DeWitt *You Do Take It With You*, The Citadel Press, New York, 1955.

Murphy, Gardner "Three Papers on the Survival Problem," American Society for Psychical Research, New York.

Penfield, Wilder "The Cerebral Cortex of the Mind of Man," *Physical Basis of Mind*, (Ed.) Peter Laslett, Oxford, 1950.

———— "Some Observations on the Functional Organization of the Human Brain," American Philosophical Society, Philadelphia, 1954.

Time Magazine, January 11, 1963, "Can Man Learn to Use the Other Half of His Brain?"

CHAPTER 6   TRAVELLING CLAIRVOYANCE

Cornellier, Pierre Emile   *Journal,* S.P.R., Vol. XXI.

Eastman, Margaret   "Out-of-the-Body Experiences," *Proceedings,* S.P.R., Vol. 53, December, 1962.

Edmunds, Simeon   "The Higher Phenomena of Hypnotism," *Tomorrow,* Autumn, 1963, Vol. II, No. 4.

Fahler, Jarl   "Does Hypnosis Increase Psychic Power?" *Tomorrow,* Autumn, 1958, Vol. 6, No. 4.

Fate Magazine, July, 1963, Vol. 16, No. 7.

Garrett, Eileen J. "The Nature of My Controls," *Tomorrow,* Autumn, 1963, Vol. II, No. 4.

———— *My Life as a Search for the Meaning of Mediumship,* Rider & Co., London, 1939.

Prince, Walter Franklin *Noted Witnesses for Psychic Occurrences,* University Books, New York, 1963.

Sidgwick, Eleanor   "On the Evidence for Clairvoyance," *Proceedings,* S.P.R., Vol. VII, pp. 30-99.

CHAPTER 7   ESP PROJECTIONS

Crookall, Robert   "Astral Travelling," *Journal,* S.P.R., September, 1963.

Gurney, Podmore, Myers *Phantasms of the Living,* University Books, New York, 1962.

Myers, F. W. H.   *Human Personality and Its Survival of Bodily Death,* University Books, New York, 1961. (Ed. by Susy Smith).

Owen, G. Vale   *Facts and the Future Life,* Hutchinson & Co., London, 1922.

CHAPTER 8   THE HUMAN DOUBLE

Ducasse, C. J.   *The Belief in a Life After Death,* Charles C Thomas, Springfield, Ill., 1961.

Heywood, Rosalind   *ESP: A Personal Memoir,* E. P. Dutton & Co., Inc., New York, 1964, p. 105.

Jaffé, Aniela *Apparitions and Precognition,* University Books, New York, 1963.

Journal, S.P.R., Vol. VI, pp. 286-88.

Tweedale, Charles L. *Man's Survival After Death,* Spiritualist Press, Ltd., London, 1909.

Tyrrell, G. N. M. *Apparitions,* University Books, New York, 1961.

———— *Personality of Man,* Penguin Books, Middlesex, 1947.

Wereide, Thorstein "Norway's Human Doubles," *Tomorrow,* Winter, 1955, Vol. 3, No. 2.

CHAPTER 9   BILOCATION

Del Fante, Alberto *Who Is Padre Pio?*, Radio Replies Press Society, U.S.A., 1955.

Hunt, Douglas *Exploring the Occult*, Pan Books, Ltd., London, 1964.

Journal, S.P.R., Vol. XII, p. 193.

Thurston, Fr. Herbert *Surprising Mystics*, Burns & Oates, London, 1955.

CHAPTER 10   MEDIUMS

Balfour, Earl of "A Study of the Psychological Aspects of Mrs. Willett's Mediumship," *Proceedings*, S.P.R., Vol. XLIII.

Hillers, Henry S. "Projecting the Etheric Body," *Journal*, A.S.P.R., Vol. 29.

Leonard, Gladys Osborne *My Life in Two Worlds*, Cassell & Co., London, 1931.

Shelton, Harriett M. *Astral Flights*, privately printed, 1963.

Williams, Sophia *You Are Psychic*, Murray & Gee, Hollywood, 1946.

CHAPTER 11   CHILDREN AND PRIMITIVES

Eliade, Mircea *Shamanism: Archaic Techniques of Ecstasy*, Pantheon Books, New York, 1963.

Freuchen, Peter *The Book of the Eskimos*, World Publishing Co., New York, 1961.

Rose, Ronald *Living Magic*, Chatto & Windus, London, 1957.

Titiev, Mischa *Introduction to Cultural Anthropology*, Holt, Rinehart & Winston, New York, 1959.

CHAPTER 12   ECSTATIC STATES

Bucke, Richard M. *Cosmic Consciousness*, E. P. Dutton & Co., New York, 1901.

Dunlap, Jane *Exploring Inner Space*, Harcourt, Brace & World, Inc., New York, 1961.

Smythe, F. S. *The Spirit of the Hills*, Hodder & Stoughton, London, 1937.

CHAPTER 13   THE PSYCHIC ETHER

David-Neel, Alexandra *With Mystics & Magicians in Tibet*, University Books, New York, 1957.

Ducasse, C. J. *A Philosophical Scrutiny of Religion*, The Ronald Press Co., New York, 1953.

Johnson, Raynor C. *Nurslings of Immortality*, Harper & Bros., New York, 1957.

Jourdain, E. F., and Moberly, C. A. E. *An Adventure*, Coward McCann, New York, 1955.

Journal, S.P.R., Vol. 36, 1951.

Sherman, Harold *How To Make ESP Work For You*, DeVorss & Co., Inc., Los Angeles, 1964, p. 52.

CHAPTER 14   CLOSE CALLS AND PERMANENT PROJECTIONS

Guideposts, June, 1963.

Journal, S. P. R., Vol. XIX, p. 76.

———, Vol. XVII, p. 230.

Proceedings, S. P. R., Vol. I, p. 122.

CHAPTER 15 THE FAINTLY-GLOWING MIST

Bozzano, Ernesto *Discarnate Influence in Human Life* John M. Watkins, London (no date).

Ducasse, C. J. *The Belief in a Life After Death,* Charles C Thomas, Springfield, Illinois, 1960.

Hart, Hornell, "Six Theories About Apparitions," *Proceedings,* S. P. R., Vol. 50, May, 1956.

Light, 1922.

CHAPTER 16 THE GREATEST CASE OF ALL

Hodgson, Richard *Religio-Philosophical Journal,* December 20, 1890.

Stevens, E. W. pamphlet "The Watseka Wonder," Religio-Philosophical Publishing House, Chicago, 1887.

CHAPTER 17 FINALE

Landau, Lucien "An Unusual Out-of-Body Experience," *Journal,* S. P. R., Vol. 42, September, 1963.

Murphy, Gardner *Challenge of Psychical Research,* Harper and Bros., New York, 1961.

ADDITIONAL BIBLIOGRAPHY

Battersby, H. F. P. *Man Outside Himself,* Rider & Co., London.

Bouissou, Michael *The Life of a Sensitive,* Sidgwick & Jackson, London, 1955.

Carrel, Alexis *Man the Unknown,* Hamish Hamilton, London, 1935.

Conger, Wilda Lowell, and Cushman, Elizabeth *Forever Is Now,* The Christopher Publishing House, Boston, 1964.

Cronholm, Borje "Phantom Limbs in Amputees," *Acta Psychiatrica et Neurologica Scandinavia,* Stockholm, 1951.

Crookall, Robert *The Techniques of Astral Projection,* The Aquarian Press, London, 1964.

——— "Journey Into Death," *Fate,* June, 1963, Vol. 16, No. 6.

Ethelberg, Sven "Changes in Circulation Through the Anterior Cerebral Artery," *Acta Psychiatrica et Neurologica Scandinavia,* Stockholm, 1951.

Iremonger, Lucille *The Ghosts of Versailles,* Faber & Faber, London, 1957.

MacRobert, Russell G. "Hallucinations of the Sane," *Journal of Insurance Medicine,* Vol. V, No. 3, July, 1950.

Mühl, Anita M. *Automatic Writing,* Helix Press, New York, 1963.

Osis, Karlis *Deathbed Observations by Physicians & Nurses,* Parapsychology Foundation, New York, 1961.

Osty, Eugene *Supernormal Faculties in Man,* Methuen & Co., Ltd., 1923.

Smith, Susy *ESP*, Pyramid Publications, New York, 1962.
——— *The Mediumship of Mrs. Leonard*, University Books, New York, 1964.
——— *World of the Strange*, Pyramid Publications, New York, 1963.
Thouless, Robert H. *Experimental Psychical Research*, Penguin Books, London, 1963.
Whiteman, J. H. M. "The Process of Separation and Return in Experiences Fully Out-of-the-Body," *Proceedings*, S. P. R., Vol. 1, 1953-56.

Index

Dandy, Walter, 66f.
Dante, 131
Darby & Joan (pseudonymous authors), 48f.
David-Neel, Alexandra, 138
D'Avila, St. Theresa, case of, 117
Davis, Andrew Jackson, 161
Davis, Roy Eugene, 116
De Agreda, Maria Coronel, case of, 108
De Benavides, Fr. Alonzo, case of, 109
Del Fante, Alberto, 104, 105
De Liguori, Alfonso, case of, 103
De Maupassant, Guy, 102
De Morgan, Augustus, case reported by, 76f.
Detrich, Kay, case of, 118
Dodson, Lucy, case of, 158
Don, case of, 127
Doppelgänger, 58, 90f., 136, 166
Ducasse, C. J., 16, 98, 103, 138, 166, 168, 171
Dunlap, Jane, (pseud.), 133

Eastman, Margaret, 78, 101, 174
Edmunds, Simeon, 79
Eglinton, Mr., case of, 75
Eliade, Mircea, 125
Ellis, George, case of, 79
Emeny, Dr. Cora and Edwin, case of, 12
ESP Projections, 19, 81f., 106
Etheric body, 51f., 98
Extrasensory travel (see travelling clairvoyance)

Fahler, Jarl, 78
Fiattre, Brigit, case of, 29
Findlay, Arthur, 51
Fox, Oliver, 19, 32, 33, 39, 40, 43, 126, 137
Frallic, Mary Ellen, case of, 98
Freuchen, Peter, 126
Fullerton, Dr. Henry, case of, 12

Gage, Phineas, case of, 66
Garrett, Eileen J., 29f., 56f., 72f., 97, 110, 149
Geley, Gustave, 65f.
Gerhardi, Wm., case of, 35f., 41, 137
Gestalt theory, 46
Ghosts, 155f., 166
Goethe, Johann Wolfgang von, case of, 96
Goldberg, Stanley, case of, 23, 40
Gorique, Erkson, case of, 91
Greber, Johannes, 53
Green, Ellen, case of, 107
Gurney, Edmund, 84, 100, 116

Hales, Carol, case of, 16f.
Hall, Mrs. S. J., case of, 100
Hallucinogens, 133f.
Hancock, Mrs. Gaylord, case of, 150
Hankey, Muriel, 43, 85f., 98, 137
Harding, Bonnie, case of, 32
Hart, Hornell, 14, 16, 19, 61, 167
Hauffe, Frau Fredericka, 46
Hauntings, 140f., 166

Vennum, Mary Lurancy, case of, 168f.

Veridical after-images, 142f., 161, 164

Verity, L. S., case of, 84

Von Goethe (see Goethe, Johann Wolfgang von)

Walther, Gerda, 55

Ward, Frederick, case of, 107

Watseka Wonder, The, case of, 168

Wereide, Thorstein, 94f.

West, Edward G., case of, 82

White, Stewart Edward and Betty, 47f.

Whiteman, J. H. M., 19, 38, 39

Whitman, Walt, 131

Wilkins, Sir Hubert, 144

Wilkinson, Harriett, case of, 150

Williams, Hilda D., case of, 21

Williams, Sophia, 114

Willett, Mrs. (pseud. Mrs. Winifred Coombe-Tennant), 115

Wilmot, S. R. and Eliza E., case of, 87f.

Yogananda, Paramahansa, 116, 132

Yogis, 58, 116, 138

Yram, 19, 38f., 174

Zerla, Hasketh, 137